A TEXAN AFFAIR – VOL.2

'The Mission'

Richard Joyce

Copyright © 2024 by Richard Joyce
All rights reserved.

ISBN: 9798869142658

ACKNOWLEDGEMENTS

I'd like to acknowledge the help I have received throughout the writing of this book, from my friend, Michael,, whose painstaking editing and advice have been invaluable.

A TEXAN AFFAIR (VOLUME 2)

The Mission

Foreword

Denber is one of many small towns in North Texas, remarkable only for their similarity, lying in that verdant strip of land between the Oklahoma state line to the north and the busy cities of Dallas and Fort Worth to the south.

One early summer evening, in the year 1938, the streets still baking in the night air, there occurs an incident (an outrage) scarcely noticed by its law-abiding citizens, nor, more significantly, by the Law, which is not unused to turning a blind eye to unfortunate events such as this. The case never comes to court, and goes unnoticed in the annals of the town's records. No perpetrators are ever brought to book.

The peace is disturbed on that particular evening by a grinding roar from a shiny-green Plymouth truck accelerating up the gentle slope into the darkening Square, to the accompaniment of whoops and hollers from the cab. The vehicle makes two noisy circuits of the Square, circumventing the imposing courthouse, the cluster of drug-stores, dime stores, saddleries, and just a sprinkling of amazed stragglers heading home from a movie or a bar.

Silence returns to the town square as the station-wagon speeds off down the hill towards the shanty town, down beyond the tracks, where - as is the custom - a scattering of share-croppers eke out a scarce existence. Are those rowdy occupants in the vehicle blatantly intent on mischief or simply heading out of town to try out the new vehicle's pistons on the long, flat back-roads? We won't ever know (these are matters left to processes of the court, which, in this case, never took place); however, probably by word of mouth from eye-witnesses, we do know there were four or five in the truck (three in the cab, two on the back), no doubt the young sons of rich white farmers, out on a spree on a Saturday night.

The inebriated driver doesn't see the shape scuttling in panic across the dirt track (or if he does, how come the vehicle seems to veer fractionally leftwards - towards, not away from - the figure?). A sickening thud alerts him though, as the wing of his pick-up catches something soft, knocks it through the air, where it lands in the dust by the edge of the road and remains motionless.

'Hell, better back up,' someone calls from inside the cab. 'I think you hit that sonofabitch.'

Doors open, boots scrape on gravel, and a flashlight plays on the dented left front wing of the pick-up.

There's a muffled giggle from inside the cab and someone says, 'You sure as hell going to have some explaining to do.'

The beam picks up the motionless figure in the side of the road, inert like a dead possum.

'At least he don't stink like a skunk,' comes another voice.

'Let's get the hell outa here,' comes yet another. 'There ain't much movement in that nigger.'

All at once, they're moving fast, plunging back into the vehicle, flashlight beam probing, like the fingers of a blind man, into the darkness, picking out a wooden shack, the narrow porch, the steps, and finally coming to rest on the little woman at their base, too frightened to move, caught in the glare like a startled rabbit, negligent enough to be out after dark, foolhardy enough to be there to witness the demise of her husband.

'Hey, you over there. Yes, you.'

The shape remains rigid.

'She seen us, Jimmy,' says a voice.

'Don't worry; we'll take care of her. Let's go.'

Doors slam, the engine revs, the pick-up snarls away into the night, as an empty bottle of Jack Daniels loops onto the road and comes to rest beside the dead man.

The event passes into history, leaving a deadly secret behind, known only to a few. Bill Jackson among them.

PART I

The Pursuit

Tessa's Story (Prelude)

(*"I need to try somehow to explain why we all acted as we did; why we went so far, too far."*)

In the long vacation of '63, shortly before I returned to Hillcrest at the start of my Junior year, my mother launched a series of three play-reading *soirées*, officially, as she put it, '*to improve your young minds*', while unofficially, of course, to keep us three girls out of mischief on those long, hot summer nights.

To put this in context. From our earliest age, my mother, literature teacher *extraordinaire,* had taken it upon herself to brainwash us children with the beauties of Shakespeare; she'd insisted we see, hear or read all the major plays by the age of thirteen and steep ourselves in the poet's magical imagery. Going into my sophomore year, therefore, it wasn't Marlon Brando or James Dean I was pinning up posters of in my bedroom, but young Hamlet, the Dane, symbol of defiant youth, elusive, misunderstood, at odds with the world.

I often wonder exactly at what point in my life, brain-washing and filial duty turned into something deeper, a genuine devotion, as once it clearly had for my mother. Certainly, I believe, by the time of those 'play-readings'. I can't really speak for my sisters, but *I* always looked forward to those evenings, and was, on that final *soirée,* earnestly hoping I'd be cast as 'Ophelia' in what was billed as a reading of *'The Tragedy of Hamlet, Prince of Denmark'* - *abbreviated version'*. It was a particularly torrid evening, flies buzzing around, when we assembled on the family porch, my two sisters and I, my infuriating older brother, and a host of teacher friends, mostly professors from *North Texas State University*, in order to improvise our less than perfect way through the '*Danish'* play.

"Now cracks a noble heart, Good night, sweet Prince, and flights of angels sing thee to thy rest." It was only at the very end of the final scene of the play, when Horatio bids farewell to his dying friend, that I could contain myself no longer; my brother's indifferent, unfeeling, intonation of those lovely lines, seemed to me to show little respect either for the playwright or for all of us present, who'd done their best.

'Why can't you read it better, George? With a bit more fire? Horatio's meant to be upset; you read it as if they were on a camping holiday.' I swatted away a bothersome fly and put on my most sarcastic of voices. *'Night prince, make sure the bugs don't bite'*.'

My younger sister of course laughed at my audacity; my brother didn't. With equal sarcasm he replied, 'Don't get so carried away, 'gentle Ophelia'. I hope you won't let your passion blind you to your lover's faults.'

'I'm neither Ophelia, nor gentle, nor am I in love. And what 'faults' might you be referring to?'

'They're too abundant to list here.'

Lost for a good reply, I said, 'In my opinion everyone has faults. Even Hamlet. And certainly *you*.' The statement received generous support from the various academics who'd stopped talking and were joining in. Encouraged therefore, I added, 'In Hamlet's case, I might say, greatly outweighed by his virtues.'

My brother eyed me as if I were one of the dead bugs on the lamp beside him. 'D'you want to know what I think of *Hamlet*, Sis?'

'Not really.'

'He's very highly overrated. He's a malcontent, a rebel without a cause. If it hadn't been his father, he'd have found someone else to complain about.' The professors remained silent, clearly reflecting on the accuracy of my brother's sweeping generalization. and my brother took the opportunity to deal the killer blow, the intolerable shaft of insight. 'He's the kind of indolent guy young girls inevitably fall in love with.'

'I'm *not* in love with him,' I protested. But I was. I look back now and see that I was in love at that time with all fictional heroes, stage deaths, tragic young men, great literature in general. And it's only years later I realize how ingenuously wise my brother had been that evening, labeling me 'Ophelia'.

But to return to the theme. Following my angry protestations, one of the visiting professors weighed in on my brother's side, lending all the force of scholarship and learning to the argument. 'Sadly, Tessa,' he remarked, 'I'm compelled to some extent to agree with George. You see, Hamlet possesses a fatal flaw, he's a…' (for a moment he sought for the right word) 'how shall I put it... a maverick, unable to conform, in desperate need of something to protest about.' Still not entirely content with this learnéd résumé, he addressed a rhetorical question to everyone in general and no one in particular. 'Who was that sentimental fellow in Stendhal's '*Le Rouge et le Noir*'? You know the one. Wasn't it Julien Sorel? Melancholy, self-obsessed, hypersensitive, the very stuff of Romantic fiction.'

'I'm sure you're right, Vernon,' my dear mother interrupted at last, 'but I do wish my children would stop embarrassing me with their squabbling.'

'Not squabbling, Mother,' I protested, 'just discussing.'

But it was my unimaginative, already-old-at-twenty-five brother who got in the last word on the subject as usual. 'Young people see conspiracies all around, find endless faults with their betters, seek to topple them so they can make the same mistakes themselves.'

'And I suppose you're not young, George,' rejoined my younger sister with unexpected daring.

He eyed her disdainfully. 'Yes, I *am* young. I include myself in the criticism. I won't have reached adulthood until I'm at least… forty.'

For someone already twenty-five and embarked on a serious medical career, my brother's self-deprecating analysis seemed amazing to me at the time - still does in fact. But that was what he'd always been like: analytical, calculating, hard on himself as well as others.

'Well said, George,' exclaimed one of the professors while my mother added, 'Slightly over-bearing, George, for one so young.'

Then it happened. The session seemed to be over; the flies were becoming intolerable, and my mother was clearly anxious to bring the evening to a satisfactory conclusion and forestall any further 'squabbling'. But no. At that moment, another of the professors, Gordon Valentine, looking up as if addressing a wisp of cirrus cloud passing in the limpid sky, observed with a slightly mischievous glint in the eye 'You know, I wonder if lovely Tessa here really *is* Ophelia.'

It was slipped in so off-handedly, so unexpectedly, but - as is often the case with academics - so provocatively (a puff of hot air injected into the ether), that my mother simply couldn't resist taking the bait. 'What on earth do you mean, Gordon?'

Gordon Valentine smiled and sat back in his chair. '*Identity transference'*, Madeleine. It's quite a topic these days. Perhaps George here was righter than he knew when he referred to his sister as 'Ophelia'.

'Well I certainly hope not,' said my mother, and because nobody had any other ready reply, she added, 'Well, all right, to be fair, even if hopefully my middle daughter hasn't completely been transformed into some character of fiction, she certainly does behave a bit like Ophelia these days. Doleful, sad and moody, might best describe it.'

'Yes, she's so stuck up, you'd think she was a courtesan at the court of Louis XIV,' added my hateful brother triumphantly.

There was general laughter while I of course squirmed with embarrassment. The trouble was, I knew they were right. I'd often caught myself recently putting on airs and graces, acting out a role, just to shock them, catch their attention.

And thus, instead of drawing to a close, the evening went on and on, everyone having their own particular say on '*identity transference*', while I took no further part, but remained silently locked in my own desperate battle: a struggle nothing less than titanic, in which my very identity was at stake. *Am I indeed Ophelia?* The question revolved endlessly in my head.

I make no excuses, but I was young that night and impressionable. In the days that followed, I couldn't forget that evening and those remarks. Still now, as I write this record, and in the full light of the dire events that have ensued, I can find no satisfactory answer to the question the professor so lightly raised: *Am I Ophelia?* The answer is not easy.

Looking back, and with the advantage of hindsight, I'm sure that final 'reading' - late August - marked a milestone in my life, as I crossed the threshold from adolescence into womanhood, but more significantly, I can't help thinking the 'reading' and the strange discussion that followed were a mirror onto all that subsequently transpired between Adam and me, and how our lives became so hopelessly ensnared in the web of the Hamlet myth. Perhaps I should have paid more attention that night to my brother, the professors, my own mother. I come back again and again in my memory to that evening; it has a hypnotic effect on me.

Bridgeport, Connecticut, October 1967

Looking back

Adam, it's clear now as I look at his papers spread out before me, appears to have recorded only very little of the time he spent on Vancouver Island. Nor in fact did he write very much after that. Had Mary Cross managed to suck from him the mysterious wells of his imagination as well as all lustre and endeavour? Dire theft indeed. It's been left therefore to me, Tessa, to complete his - and Bill's - story.

In early October of this year, I moved up here to be with my parents in New England. Only a few months have passed since the dire events culminating in Texas in the late summer of this year, which have changed my life unalterably. But it's time - I realise that now. Let me try then, before memories are inevitably muddied and a shroud is drawn over those dreadful events, to set the record straight as Adam bade me, and, if possible, move on....These - which follow below - are his own notes from his diary (much of which I've managed to collect, before he stopped writing altogether and it became *my* story).

Vancouver Island, February 1967

From Adam's Diary

> *'I've heard it said that wraiths and witches from the spirit world wander abroad*
> *Seeking a second chance at life, and can so possess the soul of some poor devil*
> *That only the offices of a priest can rid them of such ravages.'*

She's put a spell on me. I've been hexed. She's hexed me.

Hexing's not uncommon. In the medieval world they were catching women at it all the time, burning them for their anti-social behaviour. There's no reason to suppose the practice of witchcraft died as we entered a more rational age. Just that we pay no more than mere lip-service to it nowadays.

Yes, I can see Mary dancing around the cauldron, throwing this and that into it and tapping into the residue of spite that lurks at the bottom of most females; she'd be the pretty one, with all that voluptuous red hair and those cat-like green eyes. I wonder if they'd have tied Mary to the stake a few hundred years ago. I begin to think maybe yes. Look, she's a whole five thousand miles across the ocean, but she's still meddling in my life, contriving to keep a finger in the pie. How come, if not by witchcraft? It's a feat of enormous potency and vindictiveness she performs.

She and I pass the day in telepathic phone conversations. We talk to each other across the ether, wirelessly. It's almost ceaseless. I had a conversation with her this morning in my bathroom (that most private of places, where one can go each break-of-day to meet oneself, freshen up. Yes, she's even broken into that intimate space).

I dread these 'conversations'; I just know they're going to be full of bitterness and recriminations, but I can't resist picking up the receiver. *'Don't pick up. Whatever else you do, don't pick up'*, exclaims my inner voice. But I do, and then of course it's me who must do the talking. *'How are you, Mary? I wish you were here. I really do wish you were here. It's a melancholy morning and I'd love to share the day with you. What did we do that made such simple things impossible?'*

She gives no reply. I wonder if I should tell her about how I've been meaning to write, but…

'Mary, I just can't make my mind up; one minute I decide yes, I'm going to pick up pen and paper, say sorry, ask if we can start again; the next minute I'm digging in my heels, blaming you for all our mishaps.'

'That was always the trouble with you, Adam. You could never make up your mind about anything.'

'That's just not true. It wasn't like that. I did decide. I knew I couldn't do without you; I made plans; you just refused to see them, for all the glitz and glamour in your life.'

'Why didn't you tell me them then? Why for heaven's sake didn't you propose to me for example?'

'I wish I knew. I suppose I believed lovers like us would somehow just anticipate each other's desires and dreams.'

'I'm afraid I'm too straightforward for that. Women like to know where they stand.'

I don't tell her that I dread she might regard any letter, any communication from me, as a sign of weakness, and that by remaining strong and silent, I can still at least keep a slim hope of reconciliation alive. Does she aim to swallow up even my pride along with everything else?

But across the clairvoyance of telepathy she homes in on my thoughts anyway.

'Of course I wouldn't take a letter as a sign of weakness. And as for your precious pride. Was it pride then wouldn't permit you to propose to me?'

'No, no, it wasn't that. I didn't think we needed proposals and acceptances; we were so deep in together.'

'Of course a woman needs a proposal. I would've had to wait an eternity for one from you.'

'Would you have accepted?'

'That was for you to find out.'

Round and round goes the vicious circle, in endless repetition. Yes, repetition is a feature of these telepathic recriminations. Just as it is apparently with madness too. Like a record that's got stuck. And so too is indecision. I don't know what I want to be anymore, or where I want to be anymore. I don't know anything anymore. The route that once stretched so clearly ahead of me is obscured now by twists and turns. Should I remain on this rain-soaked island? Or go back to England? Or Texas? I can't afford any more mistakes, and fear of mistake forces me into deciding nothing. I'm on a dual highway; two separate voices occupy my soul. *Zwei Seelen wohnen, ach, in meiner Brust* (How well I understand that saying now). Or is it three voices, or even four? I'm no longer sole master of my own destiny.

I'm assailed by myriads of voices all clamouring to be heard: that casual female who shares my occasional bed and challenges me to gratify her; and again, my unscrupulous boss pressing me to reward to my students ever more unrealistic grades; the slant-eyed wolf that eyes me every evening from behind a pine tree and dares me raise my chin and expose my throat; the spectre of my dead friend, Bill, who comes in my nightly dreams and summons me to avenge him (dire thought that I should ever forget!); even the wagging Labrador on the games field demands a pat from me.

Yes, to each and every one of these voices I respond, paying heed to all save the honest one in my own heart. I'm a squirrel, startled by the slightest sound. I'm a Kray twin seeing hedgehogs in the sky. And over and above it all, that one bewitching voice from across the sea, urging me to '*pick-up*'.

Don't pick up. It's a false companion. Only in my diary can I find any sort of peace, because therein lies the truth.

However, mercifully, into this pig-swill of my life, this neutrality, this survival merely, has ventured, unbidden, a living, hopeful voice. January has become February and an old friend has appeared miraculously this week on the Island. What invisible hand has washed him up on these distant shores of mine? By chance? Who can tell? Occurrences in this despotic world are all too arbitrary for that I should contrive to make sense of them.

Father Hammond, my smiling, priestly friend and colleague from the days so many months ago in that monastic school in England, which they humorously named *Desolation Island.* He, among all the priests in that drear place, had been the only one to smile. The rest, with their sour and solemn faces, had already given long-term notice that the world is but a transit-station, an unsmiling, purgatorial transit-station to be endured but not enjoyed. Father Andrew Hammond though, and I, had together smiled our way through that Purgatory; we'd stood on muddy fields together, coaching boys in football and rugby, drunk our beers in the neighbouring pub, talked with each other late into the oppressive night. Andrew Hammond had been my link to sanity during that time.

I recognised him now straightaway, that tall, gangly figure standing on the foggy dock at the Nanaimo ferry port, black briefcase clutched in his right hand, looking nothing less than a doctor, a doctor of souls, an exorcist, come to deliver some poor wretch from his evil spirits. Rid me maybe of mine?

He'd written to me a week before, informing me he was on his way to a Retreat in the capital, Victoria, and would go out of his way to stop off at Nanaimo for a few minutes, to see me if I wished. More time, he wrote, he didn't have. His schedule was tight.

I'd replied that I'd be there at the ferry port. And now, here came my old friend, that familiar figure with the constant, gentle smile (the kind of mischievous smile that says 'I've a joke to tell you'), striding serenely through the other bustling passengers, looking already strangely out of place in this drab, unsophisticated world I now inhabit. What mysterious aura lies always like a soft cloak around Father Hammond?

We found a seat in the ill-lit terminal, drank a coffee, made small-talk about the rugby in England, the league tables, trying to break each other's ice, re-establish contact. Finally he asked me about myself, my work here. I told him about the 'voices', about Mary, my loneliness, and I watched his brow furrow for a second. Then came that mischievous smile suffusing his face, and he said softly (because that was the whole nature of his voice and manner), 'In religion, Adam, you'll only hear one voice; I can assure you.' I didn't reply and he sensed I was lost for anything to say, that the ground he was now treading on was unknown territory for me. 'Believe me, Adam,' he continued, 'we're all on a journey; yours is no different. None of us can know where it might lead.' He hesitated a moment, clearly wondering if he'd said enough, and then continued, 'It's really just a matter of how steadfast you can be.'

'It's less like a journey,' I said, 'and more like a dark tunnel, with no light at the end of it.'

He just chuckled. 'There's more light than you can imagine, my good friend.' Again, I had no reply, and I think he understood my doubt, because he added, 'We can help each other, you know. People are important. We do all need each other.'

Involuntarily I wanted to reply, '*Yes, but people are merely voices, just more of the same...*', but he was already glancing at his watch and getting up from the table. 'I've got to be going. I said fifteen minutes and I really meant it. I'm expected in Victoria at seven.'

'Will you be coming back this way?'

He shook his head. 'I'm catching a direct flight to London in three days' time. I'm at *Farm Street* now, you know.' He chuckled again. 'A different kettle of fish, believe me, from those lazy days of ours at the College.'

That was it. I watched him pick up his keys from the hire-car desk and then come back to the table, and felt him press me gently on the shoulder. 'It's been great meeting you again, Adam. Take care.' He chuckled again. 'By the way, don't let your pride get in the way of the journey.'

And he was gone. I saw him go out through the door, leaving me no time to reply or wish him well. I knew I'd probably never see him again.

Where had this humble man sprung from? He'd come from nowhere, like a spirit, and then passed on, but in those fifteen minutes he'd lifted me. I marvelled at his grace, his innate abilities. I knew he was going straight to the top of his profession; Farm Street (learning the administrational skills), followed by a posting somewhere abroad no doubt, then a recall, a headmastership, and then probably a bishopric. I marvelled at his certainty, that he could be so sure. And all for what? What promise could there ever be in his vocation? None. Just blind faith in one's undertaking. And determination.

So where do *I* stand with my uncertainty, my vacillation, my self-obsession (self-pity?), my retrospection? As I walked across the lot to my car, I found myself thinking, *Don't pick up. Keep going forward. Just don't pick up.*

Now, as I write this, enveloped by the all-pervasive silence of the darkness outside, I make this vow: Let me shilly shally no more; henceforth let me fix upon my goal and at all costs not look back.

From Adam's Diary *Vancouver Island, April 1967*

Mack's written this week. Not (disappointingly) Tessa, from whom I might have expected a letter. He says he's planning to be in London during August. Meeting up with Tessa. *Would I like to join them one evening? Talk about old times over a pint of warm limey beer*. He's been having dreams, it appears (bitter-sweet irony!). Keeps seeing that moment in the mime scene when he steps forward and shoots the President. (I'm not then the only guy who has phantasmal 'visitings'). *But,* Mack finishes dispiritedly, *is it a 'President' I keep seeing or someone nearer to home, and is it really me with the gun? As spooky as hell*. But I know all too well what he's talking about, what he needs to get off his chest.

This letter has re-awakened slumbering intentions, determinations that have become already blunted again by time and distance. *Spur my dull revenge*. But, although Mack's invitation is alluring, I've put it on the back-burner. I hesitate. It has to be said, my time here has not been bad, particularly these last few months, and spring has finally come and driven away the incessant rain of winter, together with many of my 'telepathic phone-calls'. Sunnier, longer days and hopeful fresh beginnings. Do I really want to disturb those awful ghosts of the past? I hesitate.

Vancouver Island, early May 1967

Another, more compelling, voice to suck me again into the vortex. A letter from Tessa herself, precise and to the point. Echoing Mack's suggestion. *'...Would I like to meet up with her and Mack in London sometime in the Summer? Mack's coming over to London in July, and I'm of course still here. Perhaps we three could get together. Just a quick visit.'*

(I don't know whether Mack and Tessa are an item, but somehow I doubt it). Tessa '*hopes I've had a good time in Canada; wonders what prompted my sudden departure last summer; trusts Mary is okay.'* Personal, matter-of-fact things. Naïve thoughts and sentiments only. Tessa clearly knows nothing of what happened to me and Mary last year, nor of my dreams, nor even of that anguished, stark, prophetic letter of Bill's.

But these innocent communications from my friends serve to awaken in me something urgent, inopportune promptings, disturbing memories. Did I not vow, a mere few months back, to seek out Bill's murderers, lay bare the calumny, the treachery? And now, already forgetting? What do we poor, vacillating creatures have on this earth if not the holding fast to promises?

Nor, to be honest, is there anything to keep me here in Canada. This place, this establishment, is hardly worth the worry, stuck out in the backwoods of British Columbia - pine-forests, darkness, rain - offering a sorry diet of educational mediocrity. It's a weary remnant of British colonial influence. Why must the Canadians so slavishly insist on their tired British inheritance? Has no one here the wit to create a home-spun dynamic, fit for this brave new world of theirs…?

{Tessa's Story} *London, July 1967*

Meeting

Although I'd had no reply from Adam to my letter in the Spring, he quite unexpectedly rang me around that time, said he was in London, had some information he wanted to share with me about Mr. Jackson, as well as to '*touch base with old friends*'. He told me then about Miss Cross, how he and she had split up. I said I was sorry, but he cut me short, declaring he had more important news to discuss.

'Mack's over here in London. Shall I bring him along?' I asked. 'He's really keen to see you again.'

'Sure. That's fine.' Abrupt and to the point. Strangely, no reference at all to Mack's letter to him. Was it my imagination, or was this a curter, more resolute Mr. Riley? Perhaps his year in Canada had lent him a harder edge ….

*****

We three - Adam, Mack and I - sat in one of those large, noisy pubs in Dulwich on a summer evening, people milling about us happily, while Adam talked earnestly of revenge, conspiracies, violence and death. It was incongruous. He told us about the dreadful dreams he'd had the previous year in England, and fished out of his pocket Mr. J's last letter, full of its paranoia and warnings. Neither of us had seen it before, nor even knew of its existence. It was a puzzling revelation:

> 8/15/65 Austin
>
> Adam,
>
> I'm in desperate danger and I move in fear of my life. I don't know who's after me, although I have powerful suspicions, but I'm definitely being hunted. I've left Corrie and the kids for fear of endangering them, and have moved into another part of town.
>
> By the time you receive this letter I might be dead. For god's sake don't take this for the ravings of a lunatic; I couldn't be more earnest and am crystal clear about my situation. What was once (when you were here) just suspicion has become certainty.
>
> I cannot say more at this time, partly for fear this letter may fall into wrong hands. For chrissakes go back to the note, find the note I gave you. Crack the code. I think - but can't be certain - the key lies somewhere in the 'land of three rivers' and more specifically 'at the place of execution'. You'll know

> what I mean. Our mutual friend, the 'primary' Hamlet, can help you. Seek him out.
>
> I can't be more specific; it would be dangerous. Find the note, decipher it, and if anything should happen to me, deliver it to the authorities (whatever authorities you think you can trust)!
>
> Adam, your life too may be in danger; they may already be onto you. Get yourself a firearm.
>
> Yours ever,
>
> Bill Jackson.

'Does that sound like someone who's about to commit suicide?' Adam asked. He was right, it didn't. 'Tess,' he said, looking directly at me, 'you remember that night at the party when Mr. Jackson had a fit, started crying?' I nodded. (How could I ever have forgotten it?). Adam continued, 'He was afraid. From what you told me, the way you explained it to me, he was afraid.'

'Yes,' I replied, 'it's obvious why too; he was afraid of the compromising photographs, of being set up.'

'No,' Adam insisted, 'he knew nothing certain about that whole disgraceful business until later. He was afraid of something else, something much more telling; he had been so for some time, believe me.'

'Of what?' interrupted Mack, abruptly, almost abrasively. (I'd already noticed that, in the interim since Hillcrest, Mack had grown more businesslike and intolerant.)

'I don't know,' replied Adam. 'It may even have been something to do with the Kennedy assassination. I just don't know.'

'So what are you planning to do?' Mack's question was stark and uncompromising, almost provocative.

'I'm going to find out who murdered him. I'm going back out there.' There was a moment's silence as the weight and implications of this reply sank in.

Mack shrugged, trying to make light of it. 'Could I see the letter again?' Adam handed it to him and he read out loud, "*land of three rivers*', '*place of execution*'.' Why doesn't Mr. J give it to us straight, instead of wrapping it all in this cloak and dagger imagery?'

'He explains why, Mack,' said Adam. 'It's too dangerous if this letter got into the wrong hands.'

'So how are *you* going to decipher it?'

Adam grinned. 'That's why I wanted to see you guys. Thought you might help me.' He took the letter back again from Mack. 'Those first two images - what you just read out - I already understand; at least I think so. '*primary Hamlet*' still puzzles me though.'

'And this code he talks about, have you got it?'

'Yeah, that's safe; I've got the code.'

'And is it intelligible?'

'No, not at all.'

Mack shrugged again. 'Seems like you've got a cat in hell's chance of tracking anyone down, Mr. R. America's a big place.'

It came out as condescending. All Adam could reply was, 'I have to go, Mack. Don't ask me to explain.'

We all sat silent for a while as office-workers and city brokers at other tables chirped in the warm sunshine and talked about their forth-coming weekend, about sports events, the Dow Jones index.

Mack at last said, 'Mr. R, you want my advice; that's presumably why you came to see us. Well, here we go: to put it bluntly, you're going back out to the States on the trail of some mythical murderer in some fictional place, on the basis of a letter you've received from a dead man, and a recurring dream that might quite likely be brought on by indigestion.' He glanced at me for a moment, 'What's the word, Tessa? Dys….'

'dyspepsia,' I said.

'Yeah…thanks, dyspepsia.' He turned back to Adam. 'Mr. R, perhaps it's just a case of taking some Alka-Seltzer before you go to sleep.' Mack's advice was blunt, if not outright rude.

'Mack, the dream is real,' said Adam quietly. 'There's nothing wrong with my digestion.' Then he added, even softer, almost a whisper, 'Are you so sure your dreams weren't dyspepsia too then?'

Adam was serious, unsmiling, but not openly hostile. There lay, in his expression, a hint almost of resignation. I felt sorry for him and wished Mack would lay off. Mack must have realized he'd gone too far, because he gave that impish grin we both recognized. 'Okay, Mr. R, I admit I was coming on a bit heavy. Call it 'sounding you out'.' Then, almost in a whisper too, 'And my dreams, yeah, they were real enough....'

He hesitated, and I prompted, 'Well then, Mack?'

Mack struggled for a reply and finally said, 'Okay, I'm sorry. I just wanted to inject a bit of realism into this decision of his.'

Adam simply nodded and repeated, 'I *have* to go, Mack. I'm trying to make you understand I don't have a choice.' He thought for a moment and went on, 'But I'm not asking you or Tessa to come; I'm just asking for your help.' He hesitated before concluding, 'You don't know how much it means to me, your interest, your support, right now.'

Silence once more. I intervened. 'Mr. R, show me the letter again.' I took it and read out slowly, deliberately, trying to find the link, "... *our mutual friend, the primary Hamlet*'.' I put the letter down on the table. "*mutual'*, that means someone you both know.'

'Someone Adam and Mr. J both know,' corrected Mack, and added, 'Mr. Slater perhaps?' The light-hearted grin was there again.

'Mr. Slater's not going to be cracking any codes, Mack,' I said. 'He had nothing whatever to do with Hamlet. Even at the time.'

And then for just the briefest of moments a link, a possibility, flitted into my head and was gone again.

Mack finally said, 'We're not getting anywhere with all this. Okay, Mr. R, let's get practical. Perhaps I can at least help you with that. For starters, where are you going to hole up?'

'Somewhere obscure. You can get lost as easy as anything in Texas. Texoma maybe. I'll find somewhere they won't find me.'

'Fine. Next question, what are you going to do for a firearm?' He indicated the letter. 'Says here you need a firearm.'

'I don't know; got any advice?'

'Sure. Get a Colt 38 Special. If you need to kill a person at close range, that's the weapon.'

As I listened to this talk of guns, in the evening sunshine, I felt myself sliding into a cold and unreal world where death and killing were no more than just games.

'You any good yourself at shooting, Mack?' asked Adam. There was a skeptical ring to his voice.

'Sure am.' He eyed us both, as if the question was ridiculous. 'I've been doing nothing else in my vacations since I was twelve. My uncle was a gun fanatic. I spent most of my summers with him in Wyoming.' He paused, seeming for just a second to assess our interest. 'That guy used to leave me in the morning, painting a fence or something, and disappear for the whole day, and the trick, the wager, was to stop him sneaking up on you, to watch your back.'

'And?'

'Nine times out of ten he got me. Bang, bang! The guy was almost supernatural.'

'Those were imaginary bullets, Mack,' I said. 'These are real ones.'

But Adam interrupted, 'I sure could do with some of those guerilla skills. Think you could teach me to creep up on someone like that, Mack?'

'Sure could, Mr. R.'

The conversation came to an end. Adam glanced at his watch and looked at us both with that earnest expression I remember from rehearsal days, when things weren't going so well. 'Anyway, the long and short of it is, neither of you must breathe a word of this affair to anyone. For my sake and also for yours possibly.' He smiled and added, 'Not even your own grandmother, Mack.'

'My grandmother, Mr. R, wouldn't give anything away even if she were in free-fall from 38 000 feet and a sadistic Gestapo officer had just offered her his parachute in exchange for information.'

We looked at him in amazement, at that rare grin appearing once more in the corner of his mouth.

'Nice image, Mack,' said Adam. 'Is that the kind of extended metaphor they taught you at Hillcrest?'

'No, I never went much on all that airy-fairy poetic stuff. It's just a plain, straightforward statement of fact. I'm a practical person; *you* know that.'

'Then how can you be so sure your grandmother wouldn't talk, Mack?'

'Because she's dead. She died two years ago.'

We laughed, almost unnaturally loudly, surprising the drinkers at the next-door table. Adam said, 'Well even so, Mack, don't tell her. You can't trust anyone.' More laughter.

'Mr. R,' said Mack, finishing his beer, 'I've gotta be going. Listen, I'm serious; if you ever need help, perhaps training with a gun, whatever, I'll be on the next plane. You can count on it.' He shook Adam's hand. 'Don't forget, avail yourself of that Colt; you might need it.'

Adam acknowledged with a nod of the head and we watched the tall, slim figure negotiate the crowded row of tables and disappear. *He,* I was thinking, was what one calls a 'mutual friend'. Someone you know and can rely on. Hardly 'Hamlet' though, more Horatio. And then, in a flash, I got it. 'Mr. R,' (I still found it hard to call him 'Adam' consistently) 'who did you originally cast as 'Hamlet'? Way early on?'

'We never had a Hamlet. I never had a Hamlet until Earl appeared on the scene.'

'No, go back even further. D'you remember that time we were all in the library after supper - the first time the subject of '*Hamlet'* ever came up - and you mentioned someone you thought could play the part. The only person who could play it.'

'I never mentioned anyone.'

'Yes you did. I remember we all looked at Joe; everyone in the library looked at Joe Verard.'

'I certainly *thought* Joe was the only person who could play the part.'

'No, you *said* it. The person you first cast as 'Hamlet' was Joe Verard. And Mr. Jackson would have remembered that.'

Adam shook his head. '*I* can't remember that.'

'It's true. We can check with Mack.' I was insistent; I knew I was right. Joe Verard was the perfect person to crack codes.

'But I never *did* cast him,' insisted Adam.

'No, but he was the 'primary ' Hamlet.

He looked at me, still unsure. 'I'll have to rely on your memory, Tessa.' Then he added, 'Relying on you is becoming quite a habit in fact.'

We left the noisy pub and walked back to my flat. In the quiet streets he mentioned Mary, but all he would say was '*we were no longer making each other happy*'. I could tell by his looks and gestures, the gauntness of his expression, that there was more to it than just that: Mary had penetrated deeper and more surely into his heart than he cared to admit. Instinctively I knew he was in desperate need of loving; I wasn't averse to that either. I also knew that what he was planning, he couldn't accomplish alone; he would need help.

We'd drunk a lot and it seemed pointless for him to drive all the way back to W…. I asked him in, and we finished up in bed together. We made love, but in the morning, when we woke up, I could tell that Mary had been in the bed with us. It didn't really worry me; I'd expected it. I was in love with Adam; making love to him had been for a long time my heart's desire.

———

From Adam's Diary *Gordonville, Texas, July, 1967*

Alone

Yesterday, a day fraught with almost the whole range of sensations: joy, relief, frustration, loneliness, weariness, fear even, or, at very least, apprehension. I must write down a true account of my own actions now, for the record, just on the chance that the same should happen to me as happened to Bill.

I touched down at Love Field, and knelt and kissed the ground as I stepped onto the tarmac: this land, as vast and varied as a man's thoughts, and wide enough to contain wickedness and good in equal measure. My home again.

I rented a car, and found a gun-shop in a back-street of downtown Dallas.

'What kind of firearm do you want, Mister?'

'I don't know. Advise me.'

'Depends on what you're reckoning on killing, Buddy.'

'Vermin, small critters, rats, possum, skunk.'

'Then you're better off using a rifle.'

'Yes, but you can't carry a rifle around with you. They're less handy.'

I left with a Colt .38, cartridges to match, and a head full of jumbled instructions from 'Buddy boy' on how to use the little weapon. It lay on the seat beside me, compact, deadly, but reassuring. After a while, I tucked my new-found 'friend' into the glove-box; I was legal, but certain to arouse suspicion if I was stopped with a gun beside me on the seat.

I headed then straight for where I knew I'd be safe. Texoma. The thousands of little creeks and inlets that make up this giant lake would provide refuge; no one would find me there.

Gordonville, some five or so miles from the edge of the lake, just a small hamlet with a few houses spread on either side of highway 377, the old route we used to take with Bill to roll his motor-launch into the quiet water off Juniper Point. Gordonville would suit me fine. I stopped off for a milk-shake and asked the guy if he knew somewhere I could rent a room for a week or two.

'You can rent a whole house if you like, Mister. There's one right here in Gordonville, been unoccupied for months.'

I had money. A bachelor existence in the Canadian outback doesn't cost much. I could afford to bide my time, settle in. 'Who owns it?'

'You need to speak to the realtor at Pilot Point.'

'Which realtor?'

He grinned. 'There's only one, Mister. Pilot Point ain't exactly large.'

'Have you got a number?'

'Sure thing.'

I arranged to meet the man at the house itself, a ramshackle, two-level wooden structure, tucked away in the bushes some four hundreds yards off the highway. There was a porch out front with what passed as a rocking-chair; inside, two large, sparsely-furnished rooms with floor-boards that creaked as you stepped on them; upstairs, the same. Perfect. It was even quite cool in the blazing heat of July: these houses up here must be designed to funnel the morning air from off the lake through the rooms of the house, providing a natural draught.

'I'll take it.'

'How long do you want it for?'

'Initially two months; perhaps longer.'

I paid him and bade him goodbye. I was alone with my gun and the creaking floor-boards, sentinels to warn me of danger. On the bare mattress in the room upstairs, a cool breeze caressing my face, I fell into a deep sleep and didn't awake until the glare of mid-day had become the gentler glow of evening. Away off, the occasional roar of a truck passing at speed through Gordonville, or perhaps a power-boat out on the lake. No sounds otherwise except the birds in the undergrowth, also awaking from their mid-day snooze.

I was safe; who would find me here? From out of my suitcase I got Bill's letter, placed it in front of me, read it again and its coded references. '*The Land of Three Rivers*': Yes, that must be there in New Mexico, where we'd gone skiing, that vast three-sided wedge of land bounded by the Ohio, the Mississippi, the Rio Grande. Only way out, southwards. Bill had known my fascination, almost obsession, with great rivers.

The '*Place of Execution*': the giant cave up in the rocks, with its murderous and precipitous edge, where justice was meted out by the ancient pueblo Indians. Bill knew I knew that unforgettable spot. The '*Primary Hamlet*', already identified, by Tessa, as my old student, Joe Verard. She'd been right. It's true, Joe *had* been my first choice. And Bill had known that.

But what was the link binding these clues? And how might Joe be the one to solve the puzzle? Darcy's family home in Santa Fe maybe? Joe's possible grudge against Hillcrest? His innate skill with puzzles? I searched and searched in the emptiness and silence of the house there by the lake, but the riddle made no sense. What secret was there in New Mexico? I felt alone and very much in need of help.

Finally I took out the envelope containing Bill's coded message, the one he'd handed me when half hysterical in the bar in Taos, Christmas '63. I hadn't seriously sat and looked at it before.

Hateley, Faulkner, Philips, Foreman, Miller, McDiarmid, Jackson
REVEALING ST
14SQC 011022 11222212

In the silence of the evening, for an hour, maybe more, I sat hopelessly juggling the words and numbers on this meaningless message. The second line, an anagram perhaps? The seven names across the top, six of them at least recognizable as people connected with the Hillcrest School. Was that simply coincidence? What factor united them, if not the Hillcrest School? Did they, otherwise, have something in common? Four board members, one benefactor, one name I didn't recognize, and then Bill himself. I cursed the person who - as Mack had so aptly put it - felt the need to wrap a message in '*cloak and dagger imagery*'. But the creator of this particular code had presumably feared for his life, too afraid to write the plain and simple truth. I realised then that I didn't even know the originator of this message. Had it been Bill, or had Bill received it from someone else that Sunday, the day Ruby shot Oswald, November 24th? All I knew was that Bill's whole demeanour and behaviour had undergone a transformation from that date forwards.

Nothing more would reveal itself, untangle itself from senselessness, but if knowledge and possession of this message could get a man killed, then deciphering it was vital, and secrecy essential. Frustrated and angry, I put the slip of paper back in my bag and drove to the lake shore at Juniper Point. I stood in the gloom staring out over the water, watching the occasional truck snarl across the bridge into Oklahoma. Memories of Mary came flooding back, of that afternoon we'd lain here on the ground looking up into the lattice-work of trees. Across the water, perhaps half a mile away, I could make out the indistinct outline of the little sand-island, accessible only by boat, which bathers occasionally used in order to spend a private day. Tomorrow I would need to hire a small power-boat.

Back in the empty house I sat down and placed the Colt .38 on a small table in front of me. It sat, squat and menacing, staring back at me. I was here to kill someone, to deprive someone of their life. That's what the stark truth was: alone and unaided, calculatingly and with absolute finality, to avenge my friend. But then what? And how to perform the task? The simple but intrusive silence of the gun brought the enormity of the plan, the dreadful complexity of it, crashing down on my head. I was not a murderer. I'd not been trained as a killer; on the contrary, I'd spent my life encouraging communication between living people, fostering life not death. And what was I preparing to do? Deprive someone of that glorious thing I so instinctively believed in.

In the loneliness of that creaking house I experienced fear and total isolation, as the dreadful nature of the task bore down on me.

Perhaps tomorrow will be better….

*****

…I'm in exile, in this sink into which pours the misery of the world, while she cavorts with bankers, seeks out captains who can husband for her all the riches owing to her beauty. Exotic spices laid at the feet of their languorous queen…

…Was she any different from any other woman? No, except she was mine. Women rarely ever know love until they have children. Why should I be interested in her friendship? Female friendships hold nothing for me….

…Bereft. It's dark now. I have lost my sun. Nothing is as bright as once it was…. No light. It is the night of my soul, its darkest hour. I wonder sometimes if I've lost my soul altogether, but the very thought affirms its presence. No, this is just emptiness; this is hollow suffering, day after day, hour by hour, drop upon drop. And guilt, and loneliness, and bitterness, and regret, and destitution. But I'm still young….It'll get lighter soon….

…How does this leave me then with the Hamlet figure? Is it possible that characters of fiction can, in some strange way, be spirits too, seeking to occupy dissatisfied and empty husks. And am I the pursued or the pursuer?

Heaven preserve me, lest I surrender my own unique identity to a figment of some writer's brain....

*****

Today feel better, although still light-headed, almost disengaged from reality. Rather nice really. A dreamlike quality to an all-too-oppressive consciousness. The cause possibly lack of food (I lack it for want of bothering). 'Feed a cold, starve a fever' they say. But now I'm eating again...stores bought from across the bridge, in Oklahoma. Does Oklahoman bread taste different, I wonder?

Each morning, before it gets too hot, I race across to the little island off Juniper Point and practise shooting. Stand stock still, firing arm raised, one foot forward, body turned, just like my assassin in the 'dream'. Load six cartridges in the chamber and fire single shots at the target....The target: yes, I found a piece of old board down by the shore at Juniper Point, bought a felt pen, drew concentric circles and have attached the whole caboodle to a tree (hope no one finds it and starts asking questions). Thus far there's been no sign of life on my little mound of sand. Busier at weekends though, and if someone does find the target they'll probably think '*wonder who's been taking target practice*'. World is full of busy-bodies. It would be rather bad luck if it were Hateley though. That cunning and suspicious bastard might ask more pertinent questions too.

I could hit the target from 20 yards, one in six on average. Massive sense of elation on those occasions. Improvement noted. Am starting to feel almost a sense of familiarity with my hefty, metallic friend. He and I understand each other....

Evening time: Tired. I like and at the same time dislike my big, wooden house. 'Like' because it provides me with womb-like security, 'dislike' because there's no one to share it with (contradictory sensations: if you want the one, you can't have the other). I have no definite plan: I think soon I might have to venture from the 'womb' and make contact with Corrie in Austin...she'll be able to tell me much;

she'll be able to bring me one step nearer to my intended victim. The truth must out….

*****

Another day, another gun practice. 3 out of 6 now. How long has passed since my last diary entry? No date on it….A week, two weeks? Very, very negligent of me. I need a sense of time, if only to stay sane. Today, I felt both here and yet not here, could hardly move my shooting feet from their stance in the sand…body and mind on their own separate little journeys…hope they'll meet up soon. Too hot, and my wooden house retains the afternoon heat fearfully. Must send a letter to Tessa. She deserves to know my movements….

*****

Aeons have passed. And an amazing thing….I've had a joyous reunion: Mary's been here (at least I *think* she has), bossy and imperious as per usual.

She'd phoned me (delicious, peachy voice down the line) *'You might at least make an effort to sound more enthusiastic!'* Yes, a voice long extinct, explaining how she'd got two weeks leave and was coming to ….

{Tessa's Story}

Yes, but did that promised visit ever really take place at all? Adam's diary above, at this interesting juncture, remains incomplete and, in retrospect, suggests a lonely Adam finding it increasingly difficult to cope. A sense of mild delirium pervades most of his final notes, and the evidence suggests he caught a virus in the last days of July and was laid low with a fever…I'd of course, by this time, heard absolutely nothing from him and had already started to worry and wonder whether I should join him. And by sheer coincidence I received a personal letter about that time from Adam himself (along with an unexpected letter from my brother, Georges). Here follows…

Two letters

July 10th 1967 Roanoke, Texas

My dear little sister,

Your letter to us all at home has worried me. Yes, as a brother, I do worry about you, even if my manner towards you might sometimes belie that fact. I feel responsible.

You write that you're seeing Adam Riley again. Therein lies my concern. Are you sure you can trust him? Are you certain of his intentions towards you? Although he may profess love (or whatever passes for love with someone so superficial), what 'earnest tokens' has he given you, what sacrifices has he been prepared to make on your behalf? None, I imagine; and never forget, you have far more to lose in a relationship with Adam than he does.

Do you remember, all those years ago in the garden here at Roanoke, how we even then half-joked about your apparent infatuation for this man, cloaked then of course in the mantle of your heart-throb, Hamlet? (I believe I can even remember the words I used at that time to describe him: *indolent* and *malcontent* and, yes, I even remember the professor's judgement: *self-obsessed*). Believe me, that man is self-obsessed. What he was then is what he is now. I fear your dalliance (I have to call it that) can only lead you, and all of us, into difficulties. He's not the right person for you, and I suspect, deep down, you know this. He's not solid, Tessa; he comes and goes at the beck of every whim.

I beg you to hearken to someone who knows better than you do the not always honourable ways of men, and who has only your best interests at heart. Were any harm to come to you, you would not only plunge me, but all your family, into distress, and I'm unsure how I could account for my own actions in such a case. Your honour is what's at stake.... Come home.

Your affectionate brother, George.

'*dalliance*', '*hearken*', '*honour*'. As always, my dull, precise, self-righteous, censorious, strait-laced brother. Does he think this is The Middle Ages? He writes like some medieval clerk. And worse, by what self-given right does he presume to comprehend the innermost aspirations of *my* heart? I wish, I just wish, I could love my brother more. Even just simple affection would be enough.

*****

July 25th Gordonville

Dear Tessa,

I'm practising daily. I think I can manage here. I want to thank you for your help in London. And Mack. It was fabulous seeing you both again.

I have to admit I still feel split in two, the best half gone, the worst left behind. I long to have my personality back, that other one half of my soul, so I can be myself again. I wonder sometimes if the self-recriminations will ever cease, the guilt gnawing at my guts like a wild animal....

Tessa, let me confess....This past year, out of rage and spite, I have done things of which I am not proud..."we are arrant knaves all...crawling between heaven and earth...." I've made love to my neighbor's wife, I've slept knowingly with the girl-friend of a dying colleague, I've stood dates up, deliberately (and smiled at the thought of the effect), I've messed my meddling hands in other people's most intimate of affairs. What further abominations am I yet capable of...?

But I need to make a clean break. I need to atone. I've made a decision, and my way now is clear ahead. I don't think it wise for you to come out here (in case you had plans). Please understand me when I explain that if you do have to follow me, it must be on your own initiative, your decision not mine. I have nothing to offer you here except uncertainty. And danger. Have I the right to involve you in hazards of my own choosing?

Please study hard for your future. Forget me; I'm no good for you. Who knows, we may meet again one day in happier circumstances.

Yours ever,
Adam.

*****

Now, there's an irony. Two letters, one from my smug brother and another from my lover, both, in their own diverse ways, professing their concern for me, while both warning me off 'Adam Riley'. What is it with this Adam Riley? Is he a monster that I should not go near him? And what god-given right permits either of them to decide who I see and who I don't, where I tread and where I don't?

As for Adam himself, I could sense from his letter all was not right with him. It wasn't sent from the Adam I once knew, and I guessed, prophetically, *she* still hadn't really left him.

I was due in the States in September; there was nothing now to keep me in England. I packed straightaway and caught the first flight out, in search of some desolate spot on the map called Gordonville.

August 1st, Gordonville, Texas

Allies

No, he wasn't dead. But he had a very high fever, caused, I think, by food poisoning. I found him sprawled on the wooden floor of his front-room, near the desk at which he'd been apparently feverishly writing. It was likely he'd tried to get a drink or reach his bed, but had collapsed after a few paces.

I knew I could nurse him back to health. He was strong. Over the following few days, with occasional lapses into delirium, he recovered quickly and within a week he was back on the 'island', 'practising'.

As for Mary's fictional 'visit', which during the course of the next few days he refused to believe never took place (despite my skeptical looks), we agreed to drive to Sherman and check out the hotel he insisted they'd stayed at: At all the possible hotel locations anywhere around Sherman it turned out there was *no one* registered under the name of 'Cross'.

'And besides,' I said, 'how could you have done all those things you describe with a fever? Did they come here, to your house, Adam?'

'No, they never did that. It was all on neutral territory.' Whatever Adam meant by that remark I don't know, but the subject was dropped.

'I'll tell you what though,' I said, 'it's interesting, but during these last few days, whenever you emerged from your fever, you kept repeating something like *'...last temptation'*. What is this *'last temptation'*?'

'It's just something Mary and I talked about once. It doesn't matter; it's too complicated to explain.'

Clearly somewhat embarrassed, he finally diverted the subject towards me and my being there. 'But how did you know where I was, Tess?'

'I looked Gordonville up in a geographical atlas of the world in the Dulwich Public Library. Not many Gordonvilles in the Lake Texoma area.'

'But how did you know I was at Texoma?'

'You told us, at the pub, that's where you might be going. Don't you remember?

Adam hesitated. 'That could've been a serious mistake then.'

'A security one, yes I suppose. A fortunate one though under the circumstances. But guess who contacted me two weeks ago, wanting to know your whereabouts?'

'Who?'

'Charlene Mays.'

'For chrissakes! You didn't tell her, I hope.'

'I'm not that stupid, Adam. I told her I'd seen you once or twice but that you'd disappeared recently into the hinterland of London.'

'What did she say to that?'

"Hinterland, dear? I'm afraid I don't speak German, but I suppose with a name like Bellman you probably do." I mimicked Charlene as best I could.

We both laughed, and Adam said, 'Let her look for me in the Hinterland then.'

As for Adam's letter to me and his admonition '*must be on your own initiative*', when he'd got his strength back and evening came, I *did* take the initiative; I provoked him with kisses, pressing my lips tenderly on his neck again and again until he responded and we finished up in bed (best way to deal with Adam; and anyway, we were allies, both on the same side. I don't believe he and Mary ever were; that was their trouble).

Unravelling

'Adam, what are we going to do? Have you got a plan?'

We sat in the cool of the morning in the dark wooden house. No sound, very remote, just the call of birds, and a slant of sunlight trying to get at us through the south-facing window. I'd been out with Adam across the lake and we'd tried a few rounds with the Colt. It made a snapping sound as you pulled the trigger and you had to hold it steady. Strange to think this little machine dealt death. Adam was expert and hit the target at will. As we roared back across the lake, passing a few early boats, fisherman, that sort of thing, I'd asked Adam what he was going to use the gun for.

'Kill, intimidate, avoid being killed, whatever it takes.' There was a harder, more determined edge to him than I'd ever seen before. Those days, back at school, during the Play, there'd been a determination about him, yes, but it'd been slow-burning and patient. Now it was rasher, quicker, angrier; I wondered if that anger sprang partly from his recent experiences with Ms. Cross, as well as from rage against those people whom he was convinced had murdered Mr. Jackson. I realized what I could best do now was to be for him the rational voice, to formulate together a plan and not deviate from it.

Now, here in the house in the early morning, Adam answered my original question. 'Yes, the plan is to find Bill's killer or killers, and get even. Beyond that, no plan.'

(Remain rational). 'Let's think about it then; how can you be so sure he was killed? The authorities said he killed himself.'

'I'm sure because I knew him; I knew his paranoia following Kennedy's death. Something happened at that time and I need to find out what. I'm sure too because of his letter to me, and I'm also sure because of my own dreams. I can't explain to you, but they're very real indeed.'

(Stay rational). 'D'you think his killing was in some way political?'

'I can't be sure. There are two things I need to do: first, find and speak to Corrie. She'll know. Secondly, find that 'Spectre' guy, the one who tailed Bill everywhere; he must know. He never let Mr. J out of his sights.' Adam paused for a long few seconds, as if re-living some memory, and then said, 'There's a third thing: I've got to dream the final sequence, the one that'll disclose the face of the assassin. I've got to have another dream.'

We laughed. 'So, you dream on cue, do you?'

A cloud passed across his face. 'Certainly not. They're unpredictable; one doesn't order up things like that, believe me.'

'Okay,' I said, 'let's keep our plans then in the realms we know and understand. Let's do what we can do. How do we get in touch with Corrie?'

Adam shrugged. 'I've got no clue; she'll presumably be in Austin somewhere, but how are we going to find out where?'

'Phonebook?'

'Jackson's not exactly an uncommon name.'

'Then let's go to Krum; whoever's living in Mr. J's old house is bound to have a forwarding address.'

'Maybe, but will they share it with two total strangers?'

'Don't be so negative, Adam. They'll share it with *me* - innocent looking former student; I'll go.'

'Genius!'

We went, driving into Denber and out on the familiar highway to Krum. 'Don't forget, Tessa, it's hush-hush. We can't afford to be spotted. Neither of us. We'll be recognized instantly.'

'Okay, you stay in the car. These people won't recognize me. I'm not exactly famous.'

'Good-looking, though; unforgettable features.'

I laughed. 'Your features are unforgettable too, Adam.' I paused as I got out of the car and looked back in. 'Doesn't necessarily make you good-looking though.'

At the door, an elderly lady, past fifty, said, 'Sure thing; I'm certain I have that somewhere; come right on in. Former student, eh? Mighty nice folks, the Jackson's.'

I didn't tell her what she didn't need to know. After a few moments she had the address. 'Somewhere in Austin. West 12th Street, No.364.'

'You don't have a phone number, do you?'

'Sure do, young lady. I figure it's real nice, students like you calling on their old professors.' She looked at me, taking me into her confidence. 'It ain't until long after that you realize what they done for you…yes, here it is: Bill and Corrie Jackson (512) 221-4452.' She wrote it down and gave it to me. 'I hope you have success with your professor. Mighty thoughtful of you, getting in touch with Mr. Jackson. Probably had a school-girl shine for him once, I bet.' She laughed at her own impertinence. 'What did you say your name was, young lady?'

'It's Millie.'

'Well, Millie, I wish you all the best.'

Back at the car, parked down the farm-road a little, I gave the number to Adam. 'Let's go; nearest public phone box. Can't be traced there.' Adam went off and called at a phone-booth by the railway-crossing in Krum. As remote as it gets. After a few minutes he returned, thumbs up. 'Your plan worked, Genius. What would I do without you?'

'Keep on firing bullets into a piece of board and get sick.'

He pretended not to hear. 'Corrie's agreed to meet, but on neutral territory. Thinks she's being watched. She says she's taking the two kids to *Zilker Park* tomorrow; there's some kind of fair on, wants to meet at the helicopter pad at 2 o'clock. You up for a helicopter ride, Tessa?'

'If necessary. Why? What will *you* be doing?'

'Talking to Corrie hopefully. Listen, if by chance Corrie's right and she *is* being watched, then splitting up will be a good move. We'll go separately; don't be seen with me. Keep out of harm's way; take the kids on a helicopter ride while I wander off with Corrie.'

'Who's watching her?'

'She doesn't know or won't say. The same old Corrie: uncommunicative and jumpy.'

We were at Zilker Park, Austin, the following day by 2 o'clock. Adam was nervous, but clearly excited and glad to be actively doing something at last. There were big crowds, families enjoying the attractions, visiting the trade tents, going on the rides. We'd agreed to go separately just in case we were being observed, and I followed Adam, at a short distance, as he headed through the crowd towards the helicopter pad. Every ten or so minutes the helicopter landed to take on other passengers for a ride round the Fair. Then I saw Mrs. Jackson and her two boys at the edge of the pad, and watched as Adam moved over towards them.

Her first words (Adam told me later) were, '*I jinxed in and out between a few blocks on the way here. It's like being in a movie*'. Then she'd giggled, just the same as when Bill used to make jokes. Nervous, edgy. Adam added, 'There was something wrong, but I couldn't quite put my finger on it.'

From a distance I watched him behaving with Corrie as if he were a stranger, pretending to ask the way perhaps; there was no contact, no hand-shaking, no kissing. The boys registered little interest in Adam anyway; they only had eyes for the helicopter. Then Adam blew his nose - our agreed signal - and while he stayed where he was, Corrie made her way over to the helicopter pay-station with the boys. I looped round and joined her and in a couple of minutes I was climbing into the helicopter with the boys, while Corrie moved unhurriedly away from the pad. Quite some manoeuvre. Anyone following Corrie would easily have been confused by that switch.

And then, suddenly, as the aircraft swung up and away from the pad, I saw with absolute horrific certainty a face in the crowd that I recognized. A face you didn't forget. And then the helicopter leaned over and I lost sight of him in the crowd.

When we touched down on the pad 10 minutes later, I made my way with the boys to the ice-cream parlor, as agreed, and handed them back to Corrie. She was tense the whole time, found it hard to look me in the eye, and kept glancing over her shoulder, anxious to be off. Was it just plain anxiety, living alone now, two unruly kids to bring up? I couldn't tell.

'I was a complete fool,' said Adam, as we drove fast away from the Park, heading north again on the Interstate. 'I can't believe I did that.'

'What?'

'I told Corrie where I was staying. It just sort of came out. She asked me if I was back teaching at Hillcrest and I said I was shacked up at Texoma.'

'Texoma's a big place. It'll be all right, Adam. She's on our side anyway, isn't she?'

'I'm just not sure. There's something wrong about the whole business. Her husband suddenly ups and leaves, moves to another part of town and sets up house, supposedly because his mere presence is endangering her and the kids. Wouldn't you be a bit suspicious?'

'Yes.'

'Or alternatively that's not what Bill told her; maybe it's just what he told us. Maybe they had a humdinger of a row and couldn't stand each other any longer. Bill was hardly the easiest sort of person to live with. There's too many maybes.'

'Perhaps we should just keep to the maybe we know, what Bill himself told us in the letter.' I paused for a moment before asking, 'What does Corrie herself think?'

'She believes the official version: Bill committed suicide for reasons unknown. His wife believes that. The person closest to him on this earth thinks that. If I think too hard about this business, I'll start believing it as well.'

I tried to change the slant of the conversation. 'Where did Mr. Jackson move to?'

'Across town. Out towards the St. Verard University campus. He died apparently in an apartment on East Side Drive. The cops found the body there.'

'Perhaps he was teaching out there.'

'Doesn't get us any closer.'

'What does Corrie say about the move? Did they ever meet? Did they visit? Mr. J must have wanted to see the kids.'

'They never met up again apparently. It all happened shortly after he moved out.'

'Did she tell anyone where he'd moved to?'

'She says she didn't. I'm not sure though.'

We were silent for a while as we drifted up I-35, getting closer to home territory. I for one was starting to feel less nervous as we put distance between ourselves and the state capitol. There was something reassuring about the criss-cross maze of tracks that surrounded the Lake. Finally, as we came off the Interstate at Denber, Adam said, 'What I just don't get is how come Bill's 'guardian angel' wasn't able to guard him when he most needed it. What was he doing? Had he fallen asleep on the job? I remember, at Hillcrest, he was an almost permanent shadow.'

'Did you mention the 'shadow' to Corrie?'

'Yes, she just laughed and told me she'd always thought the guy was just a figment of Bill's on-going paranoia anyway.'

'That's ridiculous.' And then abruptly I remembered the face in the crowd, seen from the helicopter. I told Adam about it.

'Christ! Who was it Tessa?'

'Do you remember the incriminating photos at Mr. J's party that time?'

'How could I ever forget them?'

'I'm certain who I saw from the helicopter was the same person who took those photos. The man who was hanging around the party all evening.'

'Christ!' Adam exclaimed again. 'What did he look like, Tessa? What did he look like, both then and today, if it's the same person?'

'Tall. Lean and hungry. Like a weasel.'

'It's the Spectre!'

'Who's the Spectre?'

'The 'Weasel', Bill Jackson's bodyguard. They're the same person. The photographer and the bodyguard must be the same person!' His voice dropped down a pitch as he murmured, almost to himself, 'I always knew somehow.'

'Why would the bodyguard want to incriminate the person he was meant to be guarding?'

'Very good question. You never told me it was the same person who took the photos.'

'How could I have done? At that time, I never knew Mr. J even *had* a permanent 'bodyguard'. I was just a student, remember?' I paused, and then added, 'I hardly even knew you.'

Adam was silent for a second or two, and then said, quite deliberately, 'And are you sure you've just seen that person, that photographer from the party, today?'

'Yes, certain.'

Adam muttered 'christ' again, under his breath, and said nothing more until we reached the surroundings of the Lake. Then he said, as if mouthing thoughts, 'But if that self-same bodyguard is in the employ of Bill's father and working for....'

I didn't give him a chance to finish, but just murmured instinctively, 'Perhaps he changed sides.'

Adam swung the car over to the curb, and stopped. 'Christ. That's it. He changed sides.' He spoke quickly, seemingly to himself, 'When did Bill's father die? I'll have to look it up, but I believe it was some time in February '65. *Before* the party. Yes, that's it, before many things.' Adam looked hard at me. 'Someone got to him, Tessa. He changed sides.'

'Well, who finished up with the photographs then? That's the clue.'

'It was Hateley. It was Hateley.' Adam was looking straight out through the windshield at the road and the undergrowth ahead. 'The guy's working for Hateley. Was, and presumably still *is*.'

We reached finally our house in the woods at Gordonville, unaware that, for all Corrie's and our apparent efforts, our cover had already been blown and that the net was imperceptibly closing. Adam, although supposedly stimulated by the events of the day and by the new developments in our situation, was silent, sunk in himself. Perhaps our desperate almost fanciful manoeuvres this afternoon to conceal our identities had finally brought home to him the full realization of the task ahead of us, and its dangers: this was no amusing game, but a real and deadly contest we couldn't afford to lose. I felt helpless, knowing how out of our depth, how exposed we both were.

We ate a cheerless supper on our tiny, makeshift table, cleared away the remains, and lay for a long time silently on our backs in bed, both wrapped in the same heavy thoughts. Finally Adam broke the silence, saying quietly, 'If anything should happen to me, Tessa, promise me you'll set the record straight.'

The remark took me completely by surprise, even considering our circumstances. It reminded me too of something else, prompted a memory I couldn't put my finger on. It was a paraphrase of something else. 'Nothing will happen to you, Adam,' I tried to reassure him. 'And if it does it'll probably also happen to me.' I knew the best thing I could do to help him was to keep thinking rationally. 'But wouldn't it be a smart idea to write down clearly *now* what we already know, and deposit it with some body, some organization, to stand as guarantee?'

'Good idea. But who can we tell? And what? Right now there's nothing to tell.'

We lay there for a long time silently in the bed, each separately seeking a way forward. Finally I said, 'Adam, why did you send me that letter? The one telling me not to come.' It had long puzzled me.

He didn't reply at once, and then said, almost to himself, 'I didn't want you to get involved. This is *my* struggle.'

'Why is it just yours, Adam? Why can't you let others help you?'

'It's dangerous, that's why. What right have I to expose you and others to danger?'

'Why not go to the police and tell them what you know? That's what they're there for.'

'The Texas police? D'you mean the ones who were supposed to guard the chief suspect in a presidential assassination four years ago?' There was a sardonic ring to his voice, that old, almost theatrical tone I knew so well from the days of the 'Play'. He continued, "*The ravings of a lunatic*', that's what they'd say. '*Excuse me, I believe someone's trying to kill me and has also killed a good friend of mine. I know because I had a couple of dreams and because that same guy walked out in the middle of a play I was producing two years ago*'.' His sarcasm was almost humorous. I couldn't help laughing and Adam said, 'That's what I love about you, Tessa. You never let anything get you down. You know, I really could just plain and simply love you.' He moved across the wide bed and kissed me gently on the cheek.

'Well why don't you then?'

No immediate response, and finally Adam half whispered, 'I no longer have a heart; that's the problem.'

'What do you mean, Adam?'

'He repeated quietly, 'I don't have a heart left; that's why I can't simply and whole-heartedly love you. I'm the tin soldier.' He paused and then went on, 'I have everything else: courage, strength, reliability, honesty, endurance, but I haven't got a heart. There's a spell on me.' We lay silently together again, me, tired and near sleep, playing idly with the thought of those four strange characters on their way to *Oz*. Finally Adam leaned across and gently moved my head towards him. 'You can have my body, my undying friendship, my protection, and more even than all that if there's anything left, but I no longer have a heart to give you. It's somewhere else.'

'I don't think it's like that,' I murmured, but he ignored me.

'Don't believe people who tell you men are polygamous. They're not; they can only love once.' After a moment he added, 'That's the real reason I wrote you the letter. To try to explain just that.' I had no reply. He went on in a murmur, 'I obviously failed.' Again he paused, and then said, voice more positive, 'So what better way can a man find to fill the void than to expose himself to danger, to avenge his friend if possible? What better way....' (In an instant, I had it, that earlier paraphrase of Adam's: *...set the record straight*.... Hamlet, as he lies dying, to his friend, Horatio: *...tell my story*....It was clear now).

Adam was still talking when I fell asleep. And he was still talking when I woke up. It was the dead of night. I reached across the bed but he wasn't there. I heard what seemed to be voices in the adjoining room - that room, empty of furniture, which we called the living-room. My heart almost stopped. It was Adam's voice but with varying pitch and tones. '*Please*,' came his voice, but with desperate urgency, '*please tell me; I conjure you in the name of our friendship, unbutton your secret.*'

Something told me I wasn't in danger. Trying to remain calm, I slipped out of bed and padded across to the doorway. Adam stood there, half-turned, as though conversing on an empty stage, but quite alone. No one but him. Suddenly - and my hair stood on end - came a voice I didn't recognize, lower and more solemn, issuing from Adam, a crescendo of words reaching towards a shout, *'Death, suicide, no, it was murder; I was murdered....'*

'By whom?' came Adam, with almost unbearable urgency.

*'By **him** (almost a shriek)...it was him....'*

Adam turned abruptly, adjusted his stance, put his hand in front of his face, as if to protect himself. *'Come out. Show me your face, you disgusting piece of shit!* (moment's pause*). Aaahhhh...* (a great cry, heart-rending, echoing through the empty house. I shuddered down the length of my body). *I knew all along...I've always known.'*

Never wake a sleep-walker roughly; there's no telling what might happen. I hurried across and took him gently by the arm, all the while whispering, 'Adam, it's all right, you're sleep-walking, come back to bed.' Adam - but not really Adam - looked at me with blank eyes for a second, and then the spell seemed to break and the real Adam came swirling back up at me, as if from the bottom of a long tunnel. I got him into bed and he lay for a while silently on his back until he fell sleep.

Some time later - it was still night - the real Adam woke me and told me calmly there were now no longer any uncertainties, the final piece of his puzzle had slipped into place. No need any longer for hesitation.

I thought, *knew*, otherwise; there were still many puzzles; but I knew too that Adam had finally confronted his own ghosts and allayed his doubts.

*****

The following morning Adam was devoid of energy. He sat silently on our makeshift couch, seemingly lost in thought. Wouldn't eat breakfast. Something alien had come in the night and sucked the lifeblood from him. I had to ask him, 'Who was it then, Adam?'

He looked at me with listless eyes as if the act of talking was an unwarranted intrusion on his silence. I think part of him was still out there where he'd been in the middle of the night. 'You *know* who, Tessa.' Then after a while, he added, 'You saw him yourself, yesterday, at the Fair. It's the same person.'

The question that came springing into my mind, I didn't dare ask. '*Is it perhaps more than mere coincidence, my seeing him and you dreaming about him?*' Instead I just said, 'Are you sure?'

But there was no answer; the blank, listless eyes had returned. I wasn't alarmed; I knew Adam would rally; he was like that. *'Don't ask the patient too many questions; you'll tire him.'* I'd seen those movies before, the 'private investigator', desperate to question the witness before he croaks.

I left this particular 'key witness' and busied around in the kitchen for an hour. The entire house hadn't been cleaned for a month. It wasn't rancid; no smells, but it was just plain untidy. I swept, wiped, polished where I could, replaced the chairs, made the bed (a pleasure it would be to have a 'made' bed), and put back in the right place what few kitchen accoutrements there were. I wandered about the house checking rooms upstairs that I hadn't even been in. From one of the upstairs windows, looking towards the small community of Gordonville, you had a commanding view of highway 377: '*from whence the enemy will come*'. Down on the ground floor again, I noticed a small window open on the wooded side of the house, and tried unsuccessfully to shut it properly (the weather must have warped the wood).

Back in the kitchen, I started preparing coffee, felt a hand on my shoulder, turned and there was Adam, smiling. 'Beautiful Tessa, my delectable love, please can we have a cup of coffee and some breakfast.' Yes, Adam had returned, and although I'd known eventually he would, I felt a strong sense of relief; without his inevitable presence about the place, solitude could very easily slip into loneliness.

'Telepathy,' I said. 'I was just preparing it. Must have been the aroma.' He grinned and grabbed me round the waist and I said, 'Adam, do you want coffee or what?'

Shame-faced, he took his hands away. 'What, actually, but I'll settle for coffee.' We were two lovers again, us aligned against the rest of the world and the forces of evil as we knew them.

'We can have what later,' I said, attempting earnest, 'but first we've got work to do. Can we look at that coded message again?'

'Agreed, and I'm sorry.'

'What for?'

'For not answering your earlier question.'

I had to think for a second before remembering. 'You mean you actually heard it?'

'You asked if I was sure. And yes, I am sure; I've sort of known all along it was that shit-face.'

'That's the expression you used last night.'

'He's more than a shit-face, Tessa; he's just plain evil. An insect. Apology for a human being. Kills people for sport, for money, on a whim. No respect for human life at all.' Adam was back, with all his anger and paranoia. 'And I met him last night, remember?' (a shadow flitted across his face) . 'Creatures like that freeze the blood.'

Everyone has a right to a fair trial, even a hired assassin, but I knew it was useless maintaining that argument with Adam; his dreams were realer to him than any evidence based on facts alone. 'What are you going to do then?'

'Kill him, before he kills us. What else can we do?' Adam noticed my hesitation and went on, 'I feel no guilt in his respect, Tessa; he enjoys his killing.'

'But why do you think he's after *you*?'

'I don't know. I just do.' He hesitated for a second and then added, 'Probably because I knew Bill. We're next in line.'

'Just knowing someone; is that enough reason for killing a man?'

Adam said, 'Bill knew something he shouldn't; that's the reason he died. Now *I* know something I shouldn't. Even though I don't know exactly what.'

We looked at each other, bewildered. I said, 'Well what's the common link then?'

The question seemed to trigger something, the same reflex, in both of us. We looked at each other, almost panicking. 'Tessa, where *is* that message? The coded message?'

Moment of panic. '*You've* got it for heavens sakes! That's our life-blood.' Adam fumbled around in the desk. Found it. 'When did Bill give you this note?'

'Ages ago. It was up in New Mexico. That Christmas I spent with him and Corrie.'

'Did Bill himself write the message?'

'Again, I don't know.'

We looked at it together, willing the truth out of it: a list of names, all linked (apart from McDiarmid) to Denber, to the Hillcrest community in some way. *Hateley, Faulkner, Philips, Foreman, Miller, McDiarmid, Jackson.*

Adam said, 'We can link the first five names directly to Hillcrest; either as Board members or benefactors. McDiarmid I don't know. And then there's Bill Jackson.'

And at that moment, like the loosening of a stubborn rock, part of the truth came free in my head. 'Adam, look at these names. Which one is the odd one out?'

'Jackson,' replied Adam without hesitation.

'Why?'

'Because, with the possible exception of McDiarmid, who I don't know, he's a generation younger than the rest of them.'

'But suppose he *isn't* a generation younger.'

Adam's expression passed through the gradations from incomprehension to realisation in a matter of seconds. 'Tessa, once again, you're a genius! How stupid of me; I've just not been thinking clearly.'

'That's because you've been too busy with ghosts.'

'Don't remind me of them.' The colour drained from his face at the very thought.

'I'm sorry,' I said.

He looked at me, light in his eyes reappearing. 'It's all right. I think I've finished with spirits now, Tessa. It's time for action.' He indicated the list. 'So this then isn't Bill Jnr, it's Bill *Snr*.'

'I think so.'

'Ha ha! A scurvy crew indeed then. Partners all, with a guilty secret.'

'I don't suppose it would be too hard to find out the identity of McDiarmid either. They're bound to be local men.'

A long hesitation before Adam finally said, 'I think - it's only a hunch - I know who McDiarmid is.'

'Who?'

'It's a complicated story, and it's only a hunch.'

'Who is it, for heaven's sake?'

Adam got up from the chair, folding the message carefully. 'It's not very important actually. I'll tell you on the way to the Lake. It's already too hot in here; let's find some shade at Juniper.'

'Bring the slip of paper, Bill's message, with you, Adam. We might need it'

He put it in his pocket. Then, as we were walking out through the door, I stopped him. 'No, wait. Let's leave it here. We might mislay it, drop it in the lake or something.'

Adam replaced it in the drawer begrudgingly.

We were halfway to Juniper when he pulled the car over after several glances in the rear mirror. 'Tessa, I'm not happy with leaving that message there. Suppose we've been recognized already, suppose we're already on Spectre's radar, suppose he's down the road watching us, what's he going to do when we leave the house?'

'Follow us, I suppose.'

'*I* wouldn't; I'd get into the house and turn it over. Find the message, realise the implications. Our cover blown sky-high. Let's go back and get it, if it's not already too late.' As we turned the key to the main door of the house, that same creepy sensation of the previous night crawled up my spine. But everything was still in place. 'Let's go then.'

'Adam, have you got your gun?'

'No.'

'Take it then. It's our second life-line. Otherwise he'll find that too.'

'I always take my Colt .38 Special when I go to the shops,' he said airily, flippantly, but stuffed it nevertheless in his pocket. We drove silently back towards the Lake, lost in our own thoughts.

'Adam,' I asked, as we neared the campsite, 'how did Mr. Jackson Snr die?'

'Heart attack on a New York street.'

'Was it sudden?'

'Very, apparently.'

'Was it expected?'

'No, he was in good health.'

'Look,' I said, 'I know it's a long shot, but suppose Bill Snr didn't die of a heart attack at all. Suppose he was got rid of in the same way Bill Jnr was got rid of. He also knew too much.'

Adam didn't reply for a second or two, and then he muttered, 'It's difficult to fake a heart attack though.'

'There are poisons these days. Send the heart into overdrive.' We both sat for a few seconds, considering the implications of this. 'So perhaps he was silenced, leaving the way clear for them to silence his son. But why? That's what we don't know.'

We sat staring dully through the wind-shield at the shimmering water. Adam said, 'He's got a widow, you know. Bill's mother. She lives somewhere in San Antonio. Corrie told me yesterday.'

'We need to talk to her. Can we get her address?'

'We can get it from Corrie.' We reached the campsite. There was a phone-booth. 'Have you still got Corrie's number, Tessa?'

'Yes.'

'*You* call Corrie. She's more likely to give you the number than me. You took her kids for a helicopter ride.'

Tessa came back after a couple of minutes, thumbs up. 'Got it. Mrs. Jackson Snr's phone number.' She waved the piece of paper.

'Is there anything you can't do, Tessa?'

'Water-ski, perhaps?'

After the anguish of the previous night, I remember that day as one of sunlight and untempered pleasure. We swam in the lake, we laughed, we fooled about and scarcely thought of the clouds gathering around us, or of the inevitable consequences of those facts we'd recently uncovered. Even our conversation about those things, and our future plans, seemed one step removed from reality, as if they existed in a separate dimension. Never again would we feel such a sense of ease and well-being. The beautiful Lake had a power over us that day to dispel anxiety. I realise now, in retrospect, it must have represented for Adam a long, happy cry from that supposed (or real) visit of Mary and her parents to a soundless, joyless, empty Texoma: she and he condemned to feed off one another forever. A true vision of hell. But not so for us that August day.

'The skis are in the boat, and the boat's on the back of the car. Let's go.' Adam tried patiently, for an hour, to teach me to water-ski. I failed. 'Tessa, keep your knees together when you come up out of the water!' I tried again, almost stood up, took fright and fell back in again. On one occasion I actually got up, rode a few yards before plunging headlong into the lake and getting dragged. 'Tessa, let go of the rope when you fall, for god's sake. D'you want to break your neck?' All kinds of advice and admonitions as, for the tenth time, he circled the boat back towards me. 'Don't worry, stay calm, relax; there are other learners falling about all over the lake.'

'Doesn't make me feel any better.'

'When you're up out of the water, ride the swell; don't try to fight it.'

Eventually we gave up. 'I'm too top heavy.'

'Your weight, believe me Tessa, is in all the right places.'

'You're too kind,' I said, trying to clamber out.

'If not necessarily for water-skiing though,' he added nonchalantly.

He was pulling me up into the boat, so I put both feet against the side and yanked. 'That's what happens to complacent and condescending bastards,' I said, struggling into the boat and leaving him treading water. I pushed the throttle forward and made a giant circle round him at least twice. He was shouting something at me from the water, so I finally relented and moved in towards him.

'Something's got hold of my feet. I think it's the dead man from dead-man's rock.' His head disappeared under the water. I panicked, edged the boat into him. Still couldn't see him. Really panicking now. And then, on the other side of the boat, his face, grinning, appeared above the surface. 'Behold Houdini, the great escape artist.' Relieved, I hauled him in with all my might.

The sun was high in the sky, and we moored the boat and made our way to the camp-site and lay near the edge of the promontory. Off the point, people were bathing, fishing, barbecuing. Must be the weekend. I'd lost all track of time. Adam fell asleep and I think I did too, and when I woke up he was quietly leaning on his elbows watching a young Negro family picnicking. Without any real sense of earnest, he suddenly said, 'Just a momentary sharp bee sting on the back of the neck, followed by oblivion. It's almost something to be wished for.'

'Adam, what on earth are you talking about?'

'A long shot. It's a bit unnerving to think we might be in someone's sights right this minute.'

'What's so desirable about that?' I glanced quickly round.

'Peace. And with so little effort.' He must have noticed my dismay because he said, 'Don't worry. It's not Spectre's style. If he's going to come for us, it'll be at close range. I know that. You remember the Play?'

The scene in our play flashed though my mind, the one we'd practised so hard, so eagerly, to achieve. 'Mack's scene, d'you mean? With the assassin?'

'Yes. It'll be like that if he comes. I know it. That scene is never far from my thoughts.' He gazed out over the water before adding, 'But best to be forewarned; we'll be waiting for him now.' He lay back quietly and murmured, 'The trouble with dying anyway is that I'd have to meet that little shit on the other side too.'

For all Adam's apparent intensity, I couldn't help laughing. 'No, I don't think he'd be where you'd gone.'

'Don't count on it, Tessa. Our intuition only extends so far.'

I didn't get what he meant and didn't want to. Instead, as we lay for several moments on the ground listening to the sounds of swimmers by the shore, I asked, 'Adam, why did you and Ms. Cross fall out?'

He sat up sharply and looked at me. 'Leading question.' He thought for a few seconds and said, 'We were both driven, I suppose. But by different things and in different directions.'

'Were you sorry it ended? Do you miss her?'

'Terribly.'

'Can *I* make it up for you then?' I returned his gaze.

'Yes, if you go on skiing like that.'

'Adam, I'm serious! Don't joke. What were you driven by?'

'She, I suppose, by her conventions, and you *know* what I'm driven by.'

I said, 'Do you really have to go through with all this? Can't you just walk away and forget it. I just can hardly bear the thought of you risking your life for nothing.'

'It's not nothing, Tessa. It's for the sake of a friend.' Then he added, 'And I suppose it's for Mary too in some roundabout way.' He lay back again and said, 'I have no choice. Let's drop it.'

I leaned across to him but he'd already closed his eyes. I think he'd dozed off again. My whole being reacted against the thought of this person, this teacher, writer, scholar, athlete, with the world at his feet, compelled to yield it up to rogues and murderers. I went for a swim and when I returned he was leaning on his elbows again.

'Where've you been?'

'Swimming.'

'I missed you. Thought you'd gone and left me.'

'You *know* I won't do that!'

I could hardly bear his stubborn and stoic shows of self-reliance, his apparent refusal to really trust anyone. He knew I wouldn't leave him - I'd even told him so - but he still could hardly bring himself to believe it. Mack too had offered his help, I remembered, back in Dulwich that evening, but even on that occasion, Adam had been more ready to decline than accept. I think he'd spent too long alone, wrestling with demons.

I dried myself silently and sat down in the sun, feeling shut out, excluded. After a while Adam said, 'Tessa, do we have integration now in Texas? How does the State stand on that? Have any laws been passed? Are black people free, or are the Park wardens going to come in a minute and remove that family down there and put them in a paddock on the sand, marked 'Blacks'?'

For a moment I didn't understand what he was referring to, the question was so incongruous. Then I realised he'd been watching that Negro family again - young parents and two small, lively children - camping near us down on the beach. He continued, 'The little boy there got into trouble in the water, carried off on an inflatable; mother of course momentarily panicked, and sent dad to swim out and rescue him. They seem to me like the same as everyone else.'

'They are,' I said 'and 'yes', in answer to your question, civil rights is alive and well. Things have moved on; Congress has passed laws. One as recently as this year, in fact. Those people are safe down there; they're tolerated.'

'Not by everybody, of course.'

'No, but there are safeguards in place.'

'But just a few years ago, when I first went to Hillcrest, those people over there might have been moved on.'

'Things have changed.'

'Yes,' he murmured. 'Things are moving irrevocably out of Hateley's reach.'

'Why do you say that?'

He turned to me, leaning on his elbow, looking at me intently. 'Something jogs my memory. Something important. I can't place my finger on it. It's coming and going, like a shadow, and I know it's something vital to our search. D'you remember how Bill was so active in Civil Rights? And Hateley, on the contrary, so adverse? I heard the guy give a talk once at Hillcrest; his hatred shone through. There must have been a good reason for that.'

'Not necessarily.'

'He must have hated Bill for his tolerance?'

'Yes.'

'Was that then not motive enough?'

'To do what?'

'Kill him.'

I thought for a second and said, 'I don't think so. Bill had to have been a threat.'

We were locked in silence for a couple of minutes before Adam said quietly but earnestly, 'I saw something, Tessa, that day in Dallas. It's in the back of my mind, but I can't remember what.'

'What day, Adam?'

'November 24th,' he replied, unhesitating. And then abruptly he stood up. 'It'll come back. I think we must go. The sun's gone and we don't want to arrive at the house in the dark.' He grinned. 'There's no knowing what - or who - we might find there.'

'Adam, you're giving me the creeps again!'

'When was the last time then?'

'There've been too many times to count. How about, for starters, yelling obscenities in the middle of the night at spirits from another world?'

He laughed. 'Oh *that.*'

We hooked the boat up and dragged it slowly back to the house in the gathering twilight.

'What was that about McDiarmid - the other guy on the list - by the way? You never did tell me.'

Adam glanced across at me, one hand on the steering-wheel, the other draped over the back of the seat in my direction. 'As said, it's just a hunch, but my guess is he's in the other world too. But most likely we'll find his mortal remains in some gully in New Mexico.'

I looked puzzled but he didn't elaborate because we'd reached the house, and anyway, I'd noticed immediately that the window from this morning - the one with the faulty catch - was wide open. 'Adam,' I whispered, 'did you open the window this morning?' He shook his head.

'It's open *now.*' We sat looking, unsure what to do. 'Should we just drive away?'

'Tessa, you stay here; get out and shelter behind the car. I'll go and check it out.'

'Have you got your gun?' He nodded and tapped his pocket. He turned off the engine and got out. I expected at any second to see the Weasel framed in the window. But nothing. I followed him across to the open window.

'For chrissakes, Tessa, stay out of this!' From inside, from the adjacent room, the kitchen, came a faint noise and shuffling. We could see no one.

'There's someone in there,' I said. 'What are we going to do?'

'I don't know.'

'Let's go get help.'

'There *is* no help.'

'We can't go in,' I said.

'And equally we can't stay outside here all night.' For a moment he hesitated, before drawing the Colt out of his pocket. 'Hell, if there's got to be a showdown, now's as good a time as any.'

'Is it loaded?'

He nodded, and then indicated with a movement of his head the car behind us. But I didn't go back to the car; I stayed by the window as he opened the main door silently and crossed slowly towards the kitchen, right arm outstretched, body taut, like in the movies, like in the Play. He hesitated before, with a sudden movement, pushing the far door open with his foot and slipping into the kitchen.

Many things flashed through my mind in that split second. What would I do if Adam was gunned down? Would I run? Would I stand a chance? Was this really happening? To me? And, over and above all these questions, hovered the one over-riding thought: how could I manage at all without Adam?

There was the sound of a short exclamation from the kitchen, and then Adam's voice calling, 'Tessa, come and see who it is.'

It was Mack. Sitting there on one of the kitchen chairs, chewing on a piece of bread. 'Hi Tessa. I knew you fellows couldn't do without me. Can't anyone get anything decent to eat in this motel?'

'How did you get here, Mack?'

'Probably the same way as you did. There can't be too many Gordonvilles in Texas. Only one in fact. And it happens to be near Denber. There's one in Pennsylvania and one in New South Wales, Australia. I ruled them both out.' He sat back and gave me that infuriating, smug, complacent, arrogant grin of his.

'How did you get in?'

He indicated in the direction of the open window. 'Don't think much of your security, Mr. R.'

Mack

The following morning, at dawn, we were on our way up into the high country, the Sangre de Cristo mountains, Santa Fe, New Mexico, Land of Three Rivers, home of Joe Verard and Darcy DeNeuve, and Darcy's eccentric mother.

The arrival of Mack seemed to inject a new sense of purpose into our mission. It quickly developed a momentum of its own. Action, not just talking. Unlike us two, weighed down by so many other considerations, and with so many elusive and disquieting spirits, Mack was clear-sighted and single-purposed. It hadn't taken him long to convince us we had to keep on the move. 'We can't just sit here in this shack and wait for Weasel to come in the middle of the night and put a bullet in each of us. We'll take two cars. He won't know which one to follow, poor fellow. We'll lead him a dance, and hit him when he's not expecting it. Before he does the same to us.' He treated the Spectre with the casual disdain of a confident adversary.

Adam told him about Bill Snr's widow, our plan to visit her in San Antonio. 'We might not even get to San Antonio,' he said dismissively. 'We need to think of the here and now. Hell, we could be involved at any moment in a Spectre-inspired 'unfortunate accident'. Weasel won't give you the leisure to plough back and forth all over Texas. Following people is what he does best.'

'But he'll follow us to Santa Fe too,' insisted Adam.

'Yeah, And we'll be waiting for him there. We've got to stay ahead of him.' Adam shrugged, uncertain, and Mack continued, 'We have to take this guy out of the equation; with him dogging us, we haven't got a cat in hell's chance. Eliminate Weasel first; there is no other way.'

'And how're you going to do that.'

'I've got a plan. But it has to happen up in New Mexico; that's his home territory, isn't it?'

'To a certain extent,' Adam acknowledged, clearly reflecting on those dramatic days back in the winter of '63. 'I think Spectre was there.'

'Good then, let's hope the Shit enjoys the trip back.'

Early next morning, while it was still dark, Mack headed off from the house, some half an hour before us.

'I'll leave first,' he'd said the evening before. 'We don't need to go into Denber. I'll follow 82 to Wichita Falls and pick up 287 there. If this shit doesn't follow me, we'll at least know one thing about him: It's you he's interested in, not me.'

'What speed are you going to go, Mack? We'll need to meet up somewhere.'

'I'll try to average 60. You guys average 65, we should meet up somewhere west of Wichita.' It was agreed. 'Whichever the case, let's aim to rendezvous 5 miles this side of Amarillo. We'll pull over, pretend we're having a pit-stop. If you haven't got - what d'you call him? - the Weasel trailing you by then, he'll have probably fallen asleep on the job.'

'I doubt it,' said Adam. 'He'll be on our tail, believe me.'

There was no sign of him by Wichita Falls, no obvious evidence of anyone trying to follow us. There, we joined 287 and headed up that long, lonely stretch through the flat Panhandle towards Amarillo. Just an empty road, except for the occasional pick-up truck; not an easy place to tail anyone. We'd almost relaxed; still no sign, either of Mack or the Weasel.

And then I spotted him. Almost by chance. I'd looked out of my window to follow the fortunes of a prairie dog or some other thing that had run out in front of us, and in the wing mirror I'd glimpsed, far back, what looked like the battered Pontiac. Just as Adam had described it to me. Dull colour, hood high, as if it were cresting the waves. 'It's him, Adam. I'm sure it is. That car has its own uniqueness.'

'For *us* it does,' said Adam. 'We'll get through Claude and hopefully meet up with Mack at the rendezvous. See if Weasel stops too. Be a good indication.'

For another seemingly endless 20 miles we drove and nothing changed. When I looked in the wing-mirror, the Pontiac was still there, maintaining a distance of almost half a mile. The topography was on our side though: it was so flat, straight and unchanging that even a chameleon would have struggled to keep cover.

'He's there,' said Adam, looking now straight forward through the windshield. He was indicating Mack, just ahead in his green Corvette, pulled over on the side of the road. Unmistakeably him. He'd made no attempt to get out. 'Let's find out where Mack intends taking us now,' said Adam, almost sceptically. I think, in spite of everything, he was still having trouble with Mack's youth and inexperience. 'No doubt though it involves me and dicing with death.'

We pulled over. Mack got out. We stretched our legs, told Mack about the Pontiac behind us. We waited. No Pontiac came past.

'He's stopped too,' said Mack, looking back up the road. 'You're right, Tessa; it's him. There's no turn-off here between Claude and Amarillo, apart from the odd farm-track.'

'Got a plan B, Mack?' said Adam.

Mack must have glimpsed the traces of doubt in Adam's eyes. He gave that wide, honest grin. 'Sure have, Mr. R. Otherwise how would I have got all those A's in your French class?'

'Everyone got A's in Adam's French class,' I said.

'Ok, you're right, Tessa,' said Adam 'but don't knock it. You could all have been getting D's. Should have in fact.'

'No one's knocking it, Mr. R,' said Mack. 'We know you were a great teacher.'

We dropped the banter and Mack outlined his idea. 'Let's just test this guy's intentions once more. Can't be too careful. I've gotta be sure he's not interested in me, if push comes to shove. Okay, this is what we do; we join Interstate 40 at Amarillo in a few miles, and need to head west. So, you take the western run-on, but I'll take the other run-on and head east. You go first from here; I'll be following, cushioning Weasel. He'll watch you enter the Interstate and then he'll watch me enter it in the opposite direction. And then the poor bastard will have a difficult decision to make.'

'You'll have to double back then,' I said.

'Won't be difficult,' said Mack.

We nodded agreement. Before we got back in the cars, Mack said, 'Rendezvous. Don't forget, if all else fails, we need to meet up before we reach Santa Fe.' He checked his watch. 'That's going to be sometime around late-afternoon.'

'Rendezvous where, Mack?' I asked.

We checked the road-map. Mack said, 'We run off Interstate 40 some way after Santa Rosa and take 285 North, the most desolate road between here and the moon. We stop two miles after that turn-off, and talk again, okay?' As he got back in the car, he said, 'If all goes according to plan, three cars will take 285 North to Santa Fe. I'll be behind the Weasel this time. Should be interesting.'

'Why don't you just run him off the road, Mack,' I said. 'Run him into some gulch and even the score there and then.'

Mack grinned and replied, 'There'll be time for all that, Tessa. Trust me. Don't forget, I hate that sonofabitch as much as you guys.' His self-assurance was staggering.

Adam, seeming now almost remote from the practicalities, said, 'This Spectre's a robot, Mack. One of the new generation of robots. You can tell that by his predictability. He lacks the vital ingredient for life: imagination. You can count on Spectre.'

Mack replied, 'Don't worry, Mr.R. I *am* counting on him.'

It went as predicted, of course. The Pontiac followed us, not Mack. Then a few miles west of Amarillo we saw Mack's Corvette join the convoy again, tailing the Pontiac now, all three cars maintaining a steady speed and heading towards Santa Rosa. Spectre had clearly not been distracted by Mack's diversionary tactics.

Then, at Santa Rosa, Mack suddenly accelerated past us. Disconcerted, I glanced at Adam. 'Change of plan?'

Adam just nodded. 'Don't worry; he knows what he's doing.' And a few miles further on I breathed a sigh of relief as Mack took the turning north on 285, a straight red line on the map, but in reality a narrow trail of asphalt, high up on a seemingly endless, windswept desert of scrub and sand and rocks. It was starting to get dark. He pulled over at the rendezvous two miles further down the road. We pulled in behind him.

'Leave your engine running and the lights on, Mr. R,' called Mack. 'He might think there's only one car.'

'I doubt it,' said Adam. 'By the way, I thought you were going to *follow* us. You had us worried.'

Mack grinned. 'Change of plan. I thought we needed to get our convoy configuration right.' He indicated with his head the darkness behind us. 'Our little friend back there likes to do the following, so let's let him do it. Don't let's change his mind at this juncture, don't let's confuse him.' There was something purposeful in the way Mack said it.

'What do you mean, Mack?' asked Adam.

'Don't worry about it; I'll tell you later,' was all he would reply, and the tone of his voice suggested such reassuring confidence we left it at that.

I looked back up the road but there was no sign of another car. 'How does he know we've stopped? How does he conceal himself? How can he see us but we can't see him? It's not as though there's any cover.'

'He has a direct beam through to our brains,' said Adam. 'You're forgetting, robots can do that.'

'Not *my* brain unfortunately, Mr. R,' said Mack, laughing. '*Your* brain. He's locked in on you.'

I shuddered. 'Let's go. It's windy and horrid here. And half a mile back there's a homicidal hit-man with a high-velocity rifle, who'd like to dispose of all three of us.' I headed back to the relative safety of the car.

'Okay,' called Mack. 'We won't go to Joe's house; it's too risky for him. Follow me; we'll meet him at the city library.'

'How does Joe know that though?' said Adam.

'I called him.'

'When?'

'I made a quick stop at a diner back there at Amarillo, while you guys were ponderously luring the robot to his imminent demise.'

We laughed. 'You sure have a way with words, Mack,' I said.

'Thank Mr. R for that. He taught me all I know.'

'It's true, Mack,' Adam confirmed. 'But only some, not all. I didn't for instance teach you how to dispose of a robot that's programmed to dispose of you.'

'No. I learnt that bit from my uncle.' He headed back to his car without elaborating.

'So,' I called over to him, 'what *is* the plan?'

'Let's get out of here,' said Mack. 'I'll tell you after we've met up with Joe.'

*****

Santa Fe public library. Washington Street. Joe was there, at a table hunched over a book, Darcy opposite him browsing through a magazine. Only a few others in the library.

'Hi, you guys!' It was good to see Joe again after so long. Slightly plump cheeks and the broadest smile and best teeth I've ever seen. He hadn't changed; he looked fit and happy.

'What are you doing these days, Joe?' Adam asked.

Joe flashed him that broad smile. 'I'm doing a degree course in Electronics at the University of New Mexico. Paid for by the army.' He grinned again. 'Managed to find some organisation that doesn't have a problem with getting your wife pregnant.'

'I wasn't your wife when you got me pregnant. Remember Joe?' said Darcy.

'True, Darce, but the army didn't know that. And they didn't want to know. That's the point I'm making.'

Mack came back from the library door, where he'd been looking out onto the courtyard. 'Joe,' he said, 'we three have booked in for the night at the Old Santa Fe Inn.'

'Just down the road,' said Darcy. 'Galisteo Street. Why don't you guys stop over with us though? Cheaper.'

'Darcy, thanks,' said Mack quite firmly. 'Perhaps another, happier time we can all pay you both a social call. But it's not a good idea under these circumstances.'

Joe said, 'Why not? What *are* these 'circumstances'?'

Mack looked hard at him before replying. 'As I tried to outline to you on the phone, we've got unwanted company and we've got business to do. We can't afford for either you, or Darce, or Mrs. DeNeuve to be connected in any way with this business.'

'Sounds like James Bond,' said Darcy.

'Except it isn't fiction, Darcy. Unfortunately.'

A few moments of silence before Joe said, looking up from his chair, 'So what do you want me to do and where do you want me to do it?' There was a more strident edge to his voice, that note of impatience we all remembered from our days at Hillcrest when something didn't accord with his views.

Adam said, 'We want you to take a look at this coded message.' He produced the vital piece of paper from his pocket and placed it on the table in front of Joe. Mack added, 'And we want you to do it here, or in the hotel, or anywhere else you choose, except your own house. At least until tomorrow.'

'What's happening tomorrow then?'

Mack looked at both me and Adam before replying, 'Day of reckoning. We'll explain later.'

Along with the message, Adam had also handed Joe Mr. Jackson's final letter. Joe read it through silently and placed it down on the table in front of him. 'Seems pretty conclusive,' he said. He looked up, grim-faced. 'I'm the 'mutual friend', the 'primary Hamlet', I take it.'

'We think so,' Adam replied.

Joe quickly scanned through the coded message.

Hateley, Faulkner, Philips, Foreman, Miller, McDiarmid, Jackson
REVEALING ST
14SQC 011022 11222212

He looked up again. 'The names are obvious. They kicked me out, most of them.'

'We think they were all involved in something they shouldn't have been, Joe,' said Adam.

Joe seemed not to hear, but returned to the message. Darcy said, 'Like the assassination maybe?'

'Why do you say that, Darce?' said Adam.

'Gee, I don't know. Intuition perhaps. I remember that creepy guy, Hateley, giving us a talk at Hillcrest. I sure bet he didn't like President Kennedy. As for the rest of those names….'

She tailed off as Joe interrupted. 'Who's 'ST'? You know anybody by those initials?' Nobody did. He returned to the message, a half smile on his face now, eyes defensive. I somehow knew he was beginning to take the task personally. 'I think the letters are an anagram. Probably two words; hence the spacing. As for the numbers, I guess they're a grid reference. The army uses references like that to locate precise points on the ground.' Joe ran his hands through his hair. 'I'll have to have a bit more time on this.'

Mack said, 'Listen you guys, let's get out of here, eat something, get to the hotel.' He checked his watch. 'It's still early; we can work on it there.'

We decamped to the hotel. Had some burgers sent up. Joe sat over by the bed, immersed in the message, occasionally writing things down on a piece of paper, presumably trying combinations for the anagram. Mack went to the window once and pulled the curtain slightly aside.

'Our friend is there,' he said. 'The Pontiac's across the street.'

We sat in silence for a while, eating. There was a sense of security here I hadn't felt in the library. Adam finally said, 'What's the plan then, Mack?'

Mack gave one of those exaggerated sighs, a short intake and expulsion of breath. It was the same gesture I remembered from classroom days when somebody asked him to answer some difficult question. He looked hard at Adam and then said, 'Do you trust me, Mr. R?'

Adam hesitated before nodding. 'Yes, I think so; it depends. If you mean trust you with the job of preventing the winger from getting into the penalty area, then no.'

Mack smiled briefly and then became earnest. 'I mean, do you trust me with your life?' I felt a shock run through me as he put the question, the same shock I presumed Adam was feeling at that moment. Adam didn't answer but continued looking straight at Mack. Mack said hurriedly, the words tumbling out, 'I'm an ace with a six-gun, fast and accurate; I'm also skilled at stalking people. I learnt it from my uncle, as you know.'

Joe had looked up from his work, that sardonic smile on his face. 'Who is this mythical uncle, Mack?'

'I told the others. Someone who taught me all he knew about killing people. I don't remember him teaching me anything else.'

'How come he knew so much about that?'

'It's not important really; he just did.' Mack seemed unwilling to explain. We all waited in silence until he finally said, 'Okay. If it helps. The guy was in charge of a commando unit in the British army during World War II. He killed Germans behind enemy lines; that's what he did. They parachuted him in, he trained the local insurgents and helped kill Nazis.'

Darcy seemed to have woken from a sleep. 'I just *knew* you were German, Mack. Remember all that German stuff back in that restaurant in Fort Worth? The name Neumann and all that?'

Mack nodded. 'My father and my uncle got out of Germany in the late thirties. Went to live in England.'

Joe called across from the bed, 'I always knew you were a limey, Mack.' And Darcy said, 'And I always knew he was a German.'

'I'm neither,' said Mack. 'I'm a Yank. They moved to the States soon after the War, where I, happily, was born.'

For a minute or two, no one had anything to add. Then Adam said, 'And so, Mack, for the next 18 years, in the backwoods of Wyoming, you trained as a terrorist.'

Mack nodded. 'The guy used to bet me a dollar he could get to within two feet of me, anywhere, anytime, anyhow, without my knowing.'

'Did he?' asked Darcy.

'Never missed. I never got a dollar from my uncle.'

There was a long pause in the room. Joe had lost interest and was back to jotting words randomly down on paper, cussing from time to time. Darcy had gone silent again; Adam and I were waiting for Mack to reveal his plan, nervous about what tomorrow held. Finally Adam said, 'So where's it all leading? What's the plan?'

'It's leading, Mr. R, to my asking you to trust me tomorrow. I'm trying to explain that I know what I'm doing.'

'What's the plan, Mack?' insisted Adam, in deadly earnest.

'Okay. Here it is. You're the guy he wants; it's plain to see. So, if we're going to get anywhere near this piece of shit, you're going to have to decoy him.' Silence. We were all listening intently. Even Joe had stopped his doodling. Mack went on, 'D'you know anywhere around these parts where we can carry out our business with Mr. Spectre without any risk of being disturbed?'

Joe said, 'There's enough wilderness round here, Mack, for you to make three American aircraft carriers disappear.'

'Good,' said Mack, and I knew instinctively what Adam was going to say, because I was going to say it myself. 'The 'place of execution'. It's in Bill Jackson's final letter. *He* knew that was the place. The ancient cliff dwellings.'

'Yes, but where are they?' asked Mack impatiently.

'Near here.' Adam hesitated before going on, 'Mr. Jackson believed he'd killed someone up there back at Christmas '63.'

'Believed?' echoed Mack.

'We looked for a body,' said Adam, 'up in those mountains, but never found one.'

'Mr. J. killed someone?' said Darcy in disbelief. I think it was impossible for her to realise this was more than just a game. Her experiences were limited. Since leaving Hillcrest, she'd had a child, was expecting one more and had lived in peace and quiet with Joe and her mother. Not like us.

'He says he did, but we never found a body up there,' repeated Adam.

And at that moment I knew, just as Adam had realised the other day at the Lake, who McDiarmid was. I said, 'You think he *did* in fact kill someone up there, don't you, Adam?'

'Sort of. I certainly believe he met someone up there.' He paused and said, 'There's no proof, but I believe it was McDiarmid.'

'So where did the body go?' I asked.

'I think it was removed, after Bill had gone, by someone who'd witnessed the whole thing.'

'That someone being the guy out there in the Pontiac, I suppose,' I said.

'Most probably.'

'I'm getting lost,' said Darcy. 'Who's this guy McDiarmid?'

'He's on the list here, Darce,' called Joe. He showed her the message.

'Okay,' said Mack. 'Don't let's get bogged down in details. What's this place got?'

Adam elaborately described to Mack the 'place of execution': the cliff dwellings, the steep incline, the steps cut in the rocks, the cave and the precipice.

'Ideal for our business,' said Mack.

'Mack,' I said, alarmed, 'you haven't even been there!'

'Mr. R can describe it to me in more detail later. No problem. Now we have the 'venue', there's no problem.'

'So what exactly are you going to do?' I asked.

'Mr. R will decoy Spectre to the very spot, at the top, this place of execution, where I'll already be up there waiting. Then we'll see what's to be done.'

'But suppose you get lost or can't find the way? You've never been up that mountain before, Mack. How will you communicate with Adam? Otherwise he'll be up on the plateau alone with a trained killer.'

'I won't get lost, Tessa,' said Mack. 'I'll be there waiting. That's why I asked you to trust me.' He turned to Adam. 'Are you willing to act as decoy, Mr. R?'

After looking intently at all of us in the room, Adam said, 'If it must be, I suppose it must be. Sounds like a good plan, Mack, and we sure don't have another.'

That seemed to decide it. The die was cast. I asked, 'Shall I come too?'

'No, Tessa,' said Mack quickly. 'If it's all right with you, you stay here tomorrow or go to Joe's home and help him with the code.'

There wasn't anything left to say. Darcy sent down for some more food, while Adam and Mack spent the next hour going over the route in detail, finalising the plan, attempting to cover all bases. I couldn't help intervening at one point. 'Leave a clue, Mack, on the path up, to let him know you got there. So he could abort if need be.'

'Great idea. I will. Don't worry,' was all Mack said. He went to get some sleep, but as he went off into the other room, he said, 'Mr. R. Important. Don't look round when you're up there. Or, rather, when you're going up there. Your life will depend on it. Just keep walking. Pick up a few things maybe, stop occasionally, but don't look back. Chances are, if you do, you're a dead man. Trust me, that's all.'

He disappeared.

After a while (it was 10.30 and the atmosphere in the room was becoming strained) Joe looked up and said, 'So you guys will be off on this hazardous mission the whole of tomorrow, eh?' He seemed tired.

'Yes, all tomorrow,' confirmed Adam. 'How are you getting on?'

He wandered over to where Joe was still seated on the edge of the bed, the coded message framed in a pool of light from the bedside lamp. Joe ran his hand across his forehead. 'I guess I'm pooped. It's puzzling.'

'Leave it, Joe,' I said. 'You're tired. Look at it again in the morning.'

'Depends on when you guys need it.'

'As long as it takes, Joe,' said Adam, looking down over Joe's shoulder.

Joe indicated the supposed anagram in the text. 'This is clever. I think it's one of those anagrams that contains a clue, a meaning, in each part of the puzzle. But the clue isn't enough.' He looked up. 'I'll crack it in the morning. You can count on that. I think I'm getting there.' Then he added, 'Who wrote this? Whose work is it?'

'We don't know.'

'Then who gave it to you?'

'Bill Jackson.'

'When?'

He was looking directly up at Adam. Adam replied, 'Three years and eight months ago, in a bar not far from here.'

Joe registered that sign of his, a sign of bewilderment, a quick brush with his hand across his brow. 'So Mr. Jackson might then have created it. It's a clever piece of work. I can see him doing the anagram but not these figures.'

Joe and Adam looked for a minute at the numbers contained on the last line of text. Joe said, 'They look very much like a grid reference. Military grid references usually start like this; the first two numbers followed by three letters locate a region of the US. I could easily find out the region. I have access to the Los Alamos National Laboratory. Courtesy of my army scholarship.' Adam nodded. Joe continued, 'But these other numbers make no sense at all. What grid reference could possibly be signified by a list of zeros, ones and two's? I've never seen anything like it.'

There was, I remember, at this juncture, as the two of them pored desperately over the scrap of paper, a sense of communal dismay in the room, a sickening feeling that Joe might fail. Darcy said, in that slow, deliberate drawl of hers, 'Why don't you guys take a break; shall I order up some more food?' But nobody wanted any more food.

Then, almost as if simply to break the agonising silence, Adam said abruptly, 'I have.'

We all looked at him, and Darcy said, 'Have what, Mr. R?'

'Seen something like it. It's a long shot, but that string of numbers reminds me of some of the answers to assignments I used to give my 5th grade Math class at Hillcrest. Luckily I had the answer book.'

Joe looked up, eyes red and tired. 'What were you teaching them?'

'A load of gobbledygook. They called it 'New Math'.'

'Yeah, don't tell me,' Joe responded by reflex. 'I remember those Math classes in Junior School: base 1, base 2, base….' And he stopped in mid-sentence, uttered the word 'christ', looked up at Adam, smiling, and said, 'I think you've just cracked it, Mr. R.' He looked down again, studied the list of numbers. 'Yes, these must be written in base 3; they're not decimal at all. There's no number above 2 in it. How could I be so stupid!' He returned to the slip of paper and worked feverishly, mumbling to himself. '0…1…then it's not 1 it's 10…which is…let me see…1,2,10…it's 3.' After quite a short while he looked up at Adam. 'There's your grid reference.' Underneath the original, he'd written his version down: 14SQC 0138 4885. 'It figures. Most army grid references have the location followed by two sets of numbers, each with four digits.' He gave that broad smile and ran his hand again across his forehead, erasing all the previous bewilderment at a stroke. 'Give me some time tomorrow morning and I'll be able to tell you where your reference is, to the last inch. It's an incredibly accurate system.' He grinned. 'For dropping bombs presumably. I'll probably have to go to Los Alamos to get it.'

Adam picked up the little slip of paper. 'A reference point to link up with this ST. Is that what you think, Joe?'

'Probably, but I doubt it'll be quite as simple as that. I'll solve it for you though.' He mumbled again to himself, looking once more at the paper. 'Could be a restaurant, a house. Could even be a prison.'

Adam said, 'Let's hope it's nothing more sinister.'

None of us knew what prompted that remark. Joe got up. 'Darce and I'll be going. I've done all I can here. Tomorrow at 12. Will that give you time to finish your business?'

'I sincerely hope so,' replied Adam quietly. 'One way or the other.'

Joe shook his hand. 'Good luck, Mr. R. Remember, stiff upper lip; that's what you limeys are famous for, isn't it?'

Mixed in with Joe's sense of humour there was almost always an edge of irony, often at the British expense. I think he must have sometimes wondered how he'd ever ended up at a place like Hillcrest.

He waved to me and then came over and gave me a hug. 'Good luck, Tess. Look after this guy, will you?'

Darcy kissed Adam on the cheek. 'Good luck, Mr. R. You sure will need it tomorrow. Or is it already today?'

Joe said, 'It's tomorrow, Darce. Still not midnight. Let's go.'

She laughed, hugged Adam and said, somewhat enigmatically, and with her usual sense of the dramatic, 'We faithful five.'

They left.

At first light we heard Mack leave. We heard a car revving outside in the street. I got out of bed and looked through a slit in the curtains. 'He's taken his car, Adam. If this place is the wilderness you say it is, that snake out there is bound to see it, get suspicious. If you get to the place, and it's parked there, then abort.'

Adam murmured something I didn't quite hear.

Retribution

Adam set off from the motel about three hours after Mack, wanting to give Mack enough time to prepare himself. From the window, I was able to watch the Pontiac, shortly afterwards, reverse and glide slowly off in the same direction Adam had taken. This account of what happened at the pueblo on Tuesday, August 17th, is of course not first-hand; I was not there. I have pieced it together as accurately as I can from the various - sometimes varying - individual reports I later obtained from Adam and Mack.

Adam:

It took me about an hour to reach the site, crossing the Rio Grande at Espanola. I'd already glimpsed the Pontiac in the rear-view mirror on Highway 84. At this time in the morning these roads are largely deserted, and once I'd crossed the river and was heading south and then west on the dusty road towards the pueblo, there was nowhere for Spectre to hide. Clouds of dust rose from his car on the unpaved track as he followed me at about half a mile's distance. Didn't he realise I could spot him?

Perhaps though he didn't care, knew he didn't need to. In a few minutes, on the trail up to the cave, it would be *me* with nowhere to hide, no cover, just him following, and if I turned around, then showdown. I already felt exposed, powerless to alter things; this wasn't my plan, it was Mack's. And it seemed a back-to-front plan. In most plans of this sort - those I'd watched in countless movies - the good guy sets an ambush behind a rock, behind a bush; he lies in wait for the enemy and surprises him, takes him unawares, kills him. So what was I doing, exposing myself in plain daylight, opening myself up to attack, and handing the initiative for at least an hour to my pursuer? How could Mack be so sure Spectre would be patient and wait to reach the summit before despatching me? It was pure surmise, nothing more. *'Don't worry. It's not Spectre's style. If he's going to come for us, it'll be at close range'*. My very own words to Tessa not more than three days ago, and now, in this colossal, silent panorama of mountains and desert, this rather fanciful notion was to be put to the test for very large stakes indeed; the idea was starting to lose its lustre.

There was no other car anywhere near the entrance to the site; I glanced quickly around, wondering if Mack had tried to conceal his off the road somewhere, even perhaps among the adobe buildings to my right, but absolutely no sign. How then had he got to this lonely place? Had he even got here at all? Was he perhaps, right this minute, frantically studying a map, lost somewhere miles away on the desert roads, without a chance of warning me? On the other hand, the absence of Mack's car would work in my favour, would trigger no alerts in Spectre. I couldn't abort at this point; I had no choice but to trust that Mack had made it here. It was all just a matter of trust.

I parked by the side of the road, climbed out. High off to the east I could see my goal: the great cave and the ledge nearby. A drop from that sheer precipice would be certain death, and probably a body would lie unnoticed at its base, in the sand and scrub bushes, until the coyotes had done their work. I scrambled over the rocks by the road and found the path through the ruins, the one I'd taken with Bill so many months before. I remembered the route: just stick to the path as it curled on up until it turned abruptly east and you reached the stone steps cut out of the rock. Walking unhurriedly, it would take me an hour. I remembered I should be sure not to look back. So far as I was concerned, the sequence of events was predictable now: the pursuer and I, both maintaining a steady upward path to the top, until, at the summit by the cave, a whole new and unforeseeable chain of events. Carefully I patted the revolver nestling in my pocket.

Mack:

It was hard to get up in the morning after all that driving the previous day. I glanced briefly into the Pontiac as I crossed the road, and saw Spectre asleep at the wheel. Sleeping on the job; the guy had dropped his guard. So he was human after all; I'd never actually doubted it, even if Adam believed he was a spirit from another world.

I could have killed him there and then. Why not? Quickly open the door and send him off to that other world with a couple of rounds. But that way was just too messy, too many questions asked, newspapers full of it: '*Man dead in car in central Santa Fe'*. Police. Finger prints. Alert this guy Hateley. Not the way we wanted it. It's too easy. No, you have to be more cunning, daring and ruthless than your adversary. Risk all to win all. We had to dispose of Spectre entirely, as if he'd never been. First rule of any commando, guerrilla, terrorist, partisan (whatever you like to call him): take no prisoners. Unless of course they can be useful to you. As a bargaining tool. 'Place of execution' (great name, Mr. J), yes, but place of torture first. I know just what we'll have to do. Place of torture, *then* place of execution. We have to extract information from this guy. I wondered though for a second if Adam, too, realised this was the only way. Was he ruthless enough? What else did he suppose we were going to do with Spectre, assuming we overpowered him? Adam, I'm afraid, has too much of a conscience; he's too nice. I have to be his unpleasant *alter ego*.

I drove the Corvette to the central square, where the taxi - thank heavens - was waiting. A pity Spectre was asleep, because this manoeuvre would really have caught him off his guard, particularly at 5.00 in the morning. All these people he'd watched go into the motel and now they seemed to be dispersing in separate directions. Dilemma for him. I took my rucksack from the back seat (vital), pulled the hood of my jacket down over my face, and told the driver to take me to Espanola; I'd direct him from there.

The pueblo site, when we reached it forty-five minutes later (without having passed a single car), was more spectacular than I could have imagined. Remote, deserted, perfect for the job; the cliff-top too, and the cave, fitted all our purposes.

'D'you want me to come back and pick you up, Buddy?'

I told the taxi driver I'd be all right. He shrugged doubtfully, but left. I don't believe he'd seen my face; he wouldn't be able to recognize me again.

I had to work fast; I had to find the right spot. I wound my way up the track, disturbing from time to time some wild-life in the bushes - birds or perhaps a coyote. *Don't turn round, Adam, if something like this rises in the bushes!*

The path turned sharply east - as Adam had described. I suddenly remembered the marker, the clue for Adam that I'd made it, that I was already waiting at the top somewhere. It had slipped my mind. What then should I put down? Nothing too obvious. I felt in my pocket: yes, a handkerchief, monogrammed, a graduation present; this had a unique identity, something Adam would notice. And sentimental value too. I was fond of it; I found myself fancifully wondering if I'd get it back from Mr. R. I retraced my steps and placed the marker beside a tree just off the path.

I went on up and reached the steps. On either side of the path I'd just come up I'd noticed occasional trees, firs mostly, with strong, bendy trunks, ideal for my purpose. I wondered if there were similar trees on the summit, on that ledge. Important that. Looking up, I thought I could see some. The steps ended about a hundred yards from the cave, leaving a short trail gradually opening onto a wide flat space, with the cliff on the right and the enormous 'community' cave looking west to a range of mountains.

Find a hiding place. There it was: a couple of large rocks with simple access involving no impediments, no manoeuvres. I'd be able to slip out easily. Adam would pass, then his pursuer, and then….I hoped I'd remembered well my uncle's training.

Check the contents of my rucksack. Gun in my pocket. Fire one round now, to make sure everything's working. I had my friend's and teacher's life in my hands. Nothing could be left to chance. The shot echoed for miles around the rocks, mingling with the startled cries of birds.

I waited.

{Tessa}:

From his hiding place behind the rock, at the top of the track, Mack had a good view of the pueblo ruins far below, and the road, the 565. He saw Adam arrive at about 9 o'clock. The sun was already driving away the shadow on that side of the cliff. He watched Adam start his ascent, following the line of the path as it headed in a northerly direction from the pueblo ruins, before it bent sharply round to the east. From that point, Mack lost sight of him.

The Pontiac came up fifteen minutes later and parked directly beside Adam's car. Mack saw the tall, spidery figure of Spectre emerge and start his ascent, moving with surprising agility, darting from time to time and making use of all the cover available. Then he disappeared too and Mack waited, senses alert, focusing his vision on that little spot down the track, at the top of the stone steps, where he hoped Adam would come into view in perhaps 30 minutes.

Adam says he climbed steadily, stopping from time to time to '*lend an air of unconcern and authenticity to his business*', but never once looking round. '*I felt like Lot's wife leaving Sodom, and prayed I wouldn't make the same mistake as her'*. The pressure to turn around and confront the sneaky bastard was at times almost unbearable for him. Hadn't he, Adam, after all done his apprenticeship on the firing range at Texoma too, and probably stood a 50/50 chance himself in an open confrontation; and then there was the continual, nagging anxiety that Mack wasn't even on the mountain. He found himself increasingly preoccupied with just two words, even saying them rhythmically to himself, and clinging to them as a drowning sailor clings to a log of wood: '*Trust Mack'*.

Then he saw the marker. A white piece of cloth lying prominently at the base of a fir tree just off the path. Why not pick it up? Make it seem part of his reason for being there at all? Lend authenticity?

Better by far - if it *was* an identifying marker - that he, not Spectre, should find it.

He went off the track a few yards and bent to pick it up. It was a white linen handkerchief, stylish and with a monogram in one corner, in another the Hillcrest logo - a Phoenix rampant representing *'a new style of education arising from the ashes of the old'*. Ha ha! One of Charlene's more fanciful ideas, the handkerchief, handed out to all graduates of the class of '65, with the initials of each graduate carefully stitched into the cloth. *You would think of Hillcrest every time you blew your nose*. The stitching showed the initials MN. With reassurance and enormous relief, Adam continued up the trail towards the summit.

Mack saw Adam's head appear above the stone steps. He didn't take his eyes off the spot, even to check his watch, but guessed it must be about 9:45. The sun was already lighting the cave, and the area around, as if it were a stage. It was uncomfortably hot behind the rocks and Mack noticed the sweat teeming down his back. He watched Adam pass him, walking slowly but steadily, face tense and set in anxiety. *'I'd reached the top; there were only a few yards further to go. Surely Spectre would reveal his hand now. How close did he want to be to me? I made towards the cave, expecting at any second to feel the bee sting, hear the crack. An eternity of moments seemed to go by'*.

'Hold it right there; don't look round.'

'I obeyed the instructions'. Then a second command: 'Raise your hands very slowly. Any other movement and you're a dead man.' *'I was a dead man anyway. I started to raise my hands'*.

'I may sound young, Buddy,' came the voice 'but so was Billy the Kid, remember? And he never missed.'

'And in that moment I recognised Mack's clear, clipped tone. For the first time in an hour I looked around. Mack was standing three yards behind Spectre, gun raised at his head - that moment in the Play, the moment of assassination, seared like hot iron for a second against my brain, then vanished. Spectre stood motionless, indecisive, snake eyes desperately examining the possibilities of a way out, the robot searching its transistors for causes of malfunction. No one gets the drop on Spectre'.

Mack didn't give him time to analyse too long; he stepped quickly up two paces and hit him violently across the side of the head with the butt of his revolver. Spectre fell, but in that split second, in spite of the blow and the pain, he acted on reflex. He hit the ground, whirled, revolver in hand, eyes fixed on his attacker. There was a shot, and Adam saw, simultaneously, the revolver leap in the air and Spectre clutch a bleeding hand, an expression of pain, bewilderment, even fear, spreading across his face. *'Hit-men need never feel fear, dealing as they do in surprise attack against unwary victims'.*

'Mr. R,' Mack called, standing over Spectre. 'Quick. Search every pocket and crevice of this shit-head for any sort of weapon. Search his socks, the bottom of his shoes, his trouser cuffs, his armpits, even up his arse if you like, for any sort of concealed weapon.'

Mack watched Adam do it. 'Okay, now take his shoes off.' He indicated then with his head, not taking his eyes off his victim. 'Over there behind me, down the track a few paces and behind that large rock. There's a rucksack. Go get it.' Adam returned with the rucksack. 'In there you'll find a pair of handcuffs. Any way you like, put them on Weasel-face here.' He kicked Spectre hard in the kidney, making the man groan and turn over. Adam fixed the handcuffs behind the man's back and tested to see they were in place. 'Okay, let's drag him together to the edge of that little drop over there.' Mack indicated the precipice. The two of them hauled him with difficulty to the very edge.

Mack now came round and looked intently at Spectre, who was in a bad way, blood oozing from his wrist. 'Listen, Buddy. You're going to need to get that fixed, but not till you've answered a few questions, so let's not waste time.' He turned to Adam. 'Mr. R, in the rucksack you'll find a length of rope. Tie it firmly around his ankles and knot it. The other end goes round the base of that very convenient tree over there.' He indicated a small fir about twenty feet from the cliff-top. 'The one whose base looks as if it may or may not support the weight of shit-head here.' A look of intense fear passed across Spectre's face, over-riding even the pain in his wrist. 'Check the knot on the tree, Adam. Make sure it's real firm.' Together they placed Spectre in a sitting position, his back towards the very edge of the drop. 'Right,' continued Mack, kneeling to face Spectre. 'We can make this quick or very painful. Question one: Did you or did you not kill Bill Jackson Jnr in Austin, Texas?' No answer. *Years of training: never reply to questions. Never talk.* 'You obviously didn't hear.' Mack repeated the question. Again, silence. Mack abruptly placed his foot against Spectre's chest and pushed; Spectre disappeared over the edge of the cliff, fell a few yards and hung there, dangling from the rope, shouting with terror. They hauled him up. 'I wonder if that rope will hold against the base of the tree next time,' said Mack. 'It was pretty precarious.' Spectre, seated again, with his back to the ledge, said nothing, but was shaken once or twice by convulsions. His face was impassive; it had rarely been other than impassive. 'Did you hear me?' asked Mack. 'I can't guarantee the rope holding next time. Just nod if you can't speak.' There was a scarcely perceptible movement of the man's head. 'Okay. Here's my question again.' Mack this time set his foot against Spectre's chest, and repeated the question. 'Did you or did you not kill Bill Jackson Jnr in Austin, Texas?' From the sitting assassin came what sounded like a growl. It was only the second time Adam had ever heard him use his voice. Mack pushed gently with his foot against his chest.

Spectre said softly, 'I was acting on instructions.'

'Do I take that as a yes?' A short nod, the man's eyes looking up, almost pleading. 'Question 2 then: On whose instructions?' Spectre creased his face into a frown and shook his head. Calmly Mack said, 'Mr. R, could you lengthen that rope over by the tree say about six extra feet.' Adam did as Mack asked. 'Good,' said Mack, looking again at Spectre. 'Here's the question once more.' He repeated his question. Same response, a look of horror and a shaking of the head. 'Right, let's hope this rope holds with a longer drop. Go think about it.' Over the edge again went the hit-man with a terrible scream. They gave it five seconds and Mack called over the edge, 'Seems to be holding. D'you want to come up before it doesn't?' Whether the guy heard is uncertain; he just continued screaming. They hauled him up again. He was trembling uncontrollably. They left it for a couple of minutes, waiting for the convulsions to decrease. Mack said, 'Okay, let's not make this too difficult. Nothing to be gained by dragging this out. Question once more.' He repeated it.

This time the words came out from Spectre in a rush. 'I don't know who gives me the orders. I just get a phone-call. You gotta believe me.'

'What's the name of the guy when he calls you? You wouldn't just take instructions like that from anyone.'

'He calls himself the Wolf. I have to call him the Wolf.'

Mack weighed the answer for a while. Finally he said, 'You okay with that, Mr. R? The 'Wolf' gives this guy the instructions.' He didn't wait for an answer from Adam but turned back to Spectre. 'Okay for the time being. We'll come back to that. Are you ready to answer a few more questions?' Spectre nodded instantly. It seemed to Adam that revealing the name 'Wolf' had been for Spectre the main hurdle; any further questions were now a simple matter. Just so as to survive. 'Good. Let's do this quickly and then we can all go home. Just a few more questions. Number 3: Did you take incriminating photos of Mr. Jackson at a party in Ponder, Texas, in the spring of 1965?' Spectre nodded, almost eagerly. 'On whose instructions?'

'Wolf.'

'Question 4: Were you complicit in the murder of Mr. Bill Jackson Snr. on a New York street in early 1965?'

Spectre shook his head frantically. 'No, that wasn't me.'

'Was he in fact murdered?'

'I don't know. I only act on instructions.'

Mack took time considering the answer, and then said, 'Okay, we're nearly finished. You're doing well. Think carefully though about this one; we need the truth.' He allowed Spectre a second of speculation before continuing, 'If we hadn't managed to get the drop on you today, where would Mr. Riley over there be?' He indicated Adam.

Spectre took a moment considering the answer, and then growled, 'His body would be at the bottom of this precipice. I've told you straight and honest.'

'Wolf's instructions again?' Spectre nodded. Mack said, 'I think we've nearly finished. This Wolf guy, tell us how you communicate with him.' It was that hurdle again. That look of terror appeared once more on Spectre's face. He prevaricated. Mack said impatiently,

'Okay, question once more; it only gets asked twice, remember? How do you communicate with Wolf? Precisely.'

'I send him a telegram to a PO box when the job's done.'

'What is this PO box?'

'It's a PO Box address in Manhattan.'

'What's the number?' Spectre hesitated. Mack put his foot against Spectre's chest. 'We're wasting time.'

Spectre said, 'You write the telegram and send it to PO Box 346, 10002 Manhattan.'

'Is that all?'

'You give him a time and a telephone number where he can contact you.'

Mack thought about it for a minute and said to Adam, 'I suppose that's a personal box number at the central post office in Manhattan. Are you satisfied with that, Mr. R?'

Adam allowed Spectre to see him nod. Mack turned back to Spectre. 'You got a real friend here, fellow, despite what you planned to do to him.' He waited while Spectre nodded his head vigorously several times. 'You understand, don't you, that it's important for us that we contact Mr. Wolf? Okay, what was that address again?' Spectre blurted out the same co-ordinates. 'Good, seems genuine.' He knelt down beside Spectre again and half whispered, 'What's *your* name, fellow? What name do you go by? I don't want to know the name your mother gave you, if you had a mother; I want to know the name you use when you communicate with your friend, Wolf.' Hesitation. That look of sullen defiance crossed Spectre's face once more. It was asking too much to give away his very identity. 'Mr. R,' said Mack calmly, 'come and give me a hand with this rope a minute.'

They got as far as untying the rope binding Spectre's feet, and slipping it round his neck, before Spectre said hurriedly, his voice high-pitched with fear, 'Okay, it's Mongrel.'

'Mongrel,' repeated Mack. 'Well don't let's forget that name. Meanwhile, I think that concludes the business. Mr. R, have you got any further questions you want to ask our friend?'

Adam took a moment to think about it, nodded, and said, looking intently at Spectre, 'Did you follow Mr. Jackson up here, to this spot, at Christmas 1963 and subsequently dispose of a body?'

Spectre was confused at first, unsure of the answer, and then suddenly remembered. 'Yes.' He nodded his head vigorously. 'Things went wrong. I had to mop up.'

'What was the name of the corpse?'

'I swear I don't know,' he pleaded. 'Mister, you seem like a nice guy....'

Adam cut him short. 'Who shot the guy whose name you say you don't know?'

Pause for a moment, then, 'I did.'

Adam looked at Mack. 'That's all I needed to know.'

'Business over then,' said Mack. 'Mr. R, you'll find a knife in that rucksack. Let's cut this guy free and be on our way.'

For the first time, Spectre's face registered an expression as near to happiness as it could manage. Adam handed Mack the knife. And in almost one movement, and far too quickly to prevent it, Mack had sliced through the rope and kicked Spectre hard in the chest, sending him howling to the bottom of the precipice, 200 feet below.

For a moment, they stood and looked at each other in silence, Mack defiant, Adam aghast. Mack said finally, 'I know what you're thinking.' He paused and because Adam didn't reply, he continued, 'This guy got what was coming to him; he was a piece of shit. The world is better off without him.'

Adam didn't reply, but walked to the edge and peered over. Perhaps the man had got snagged on a branch or something. But no sign of that; far below, this person who'd haunted his thoughts and dreams for so long lay dead, bones crushed to pulp.

Mack was already clearing things up, fetching the rope, scuffing the ground to remove any tell-tale signs. 'Hell, Mr. R, you remember what he was going to do to *you*. It doesn't do to be sentimental.' He went across to the tree, knife in hand, and cut the rope at its base. He turned and said, 'My philosophy: We're put on this earth bearing no ill-will; in fact most of us naturally happy, with a certain love for our fellow-men, empathy, call it what you like. Along comes a guy like Spectre, whose sole aim is destruction, to kill you. Then you kill him first; it's simple.'

Adam was thinking otherwise, but didn't say so. *Of course it was best to rid humanity of such people; but what right had we to act as judge and executioner?* He watched Mack busily stuffing his rucksack with his implements, apparently already putting behind him the drama of the morning, unconcerned and moving on. Where had this young person come from? So clear-sighted and already so full of righteous anger?

'He loved his work, Mr. R. What's that line in Shakespeare? Something about 'employment'? Hamlet says it. I used to think it was cool.'

'*They did make love to this employment'*, quoted Adam. 'Rosencrantz and Guildenstern.'

'That's it. Precisely. That poor guy down there made love to his employment.'

Adam was thinking of another line from another play, and of something Bill had once said to him: *'Killing corrupts. All killing, whatever the motive. Even in the heat of battle and in a just cause. You can never forget the act of killing; it eats away at the soul until at last you're a hollow shell. 'Sleep no more....' That's what Macbeth is about: the canker in the soul of every killer'*. Adam had never forgotten those words. That's what Spectre had become too, and he sincerely hoped Mack wasn't already treading the same path.

'Let's go,' Mack called cheerfully, hoisting his rucksack on his shoulder. 'Let's get out of this hell-hole.' They left and headed back down the track. Mack had tied the rope on each end of a heavy branch and was pulling it behind him.

'What's that for?' asked Adam.

'Scuff the track; leave no tell-tale footprints.'

'Did your uncle teach you that one too?'

'Sure did.'

The tension had begun to seep from both of them as the full realization of what they'd done began to become clear. They were free; no pursuit; no nagging worry. There was a lightness to their steps and the sun was warm on their backs. Adam said, as they neared the bottom, 'Mack, thanks. You were brilliant and almost certainly saved my life.'

'What d'you mean 'almost'? I *certainly* saved your life.'

They drove east, away from the pueblo and towards the river. Mack suddenly declaimed, 'He did make love to his employment.'

And then a few seconds later said, 'He did *sleep* with his employment; he did *screw* his employment.'

Adam laughed and added, 'He did heartily *shag* his employment. He did have carnal intercourse with his employment in fact; yea verily, he did *know* his employment - in the biblical sense.'

'Yeah, that's right,' said Mack. 'Fucked the ass off his employment.'

'Sexually violated it,' echoed Adam. 'Gave his employment blow jobs.'

'Got laid by it.'

The tension of the morning's hideous work was released in gusts of laughter and obscenities. After a few silent minutes Adam declaimed, 'An Employment Exchange.'

'Is that the name you limeys give to the Social Security Office?'

'Yes. I wonder if Mongrel sought employment there: 'Name please?' *'Spectre. Mr Spectre.'* 'Address?' *'No fixed abode.'* 'Previous employment?' *'Hired gunman. Got any work in that line, Mister?'* 'Well, it's a shade specialist, Mr. Speckle, but we'll see what we can do'.'

Mack giggled with glee. But by the time they crossed the great river, they'd stopped talking, each confronting the enormity of their morning's deeds. Adam muttered, 'Home territory. Back from the dead.'

And Mack said, 'Mr. R, I know you still feel bad about what we did to Spectre, but listen, think about it: what else could we do with him? He had to die. We couldn't take him with us, throw a party for the guy, invite the Wolf as well. No way that would work; he'd only seek you out again.'

Adam secretly agreed.

*****

The full details of what had happened at the pueblo I never knew until some months later. And then largely from Mack; Adam rarely spoke of it again.

When they knocked on the door and walked in that morning, we were all so elated that it was only later I realised how distant they seemed, as if they alone had shared something we could never be a part of.

'You guys look as if you've been communing with the Indians,' said Joe, clearly noticing the same, and putting his finger on it as usual. All Adam would reply was, 'It would be hard not to commune with your ancestors at a place like that.'

'So are we safe or not?' I asked.

'Don't worry, Tessa,' replied Mack. 'Spectre won't trouble us anymore. You can go about your normal business.'

The implications of that remark were, I suppose, obvious, but none of us seemed willing to confront them or to face the consequences of what we'd embarked on; so we didn't talk about it further.

'Don't you guys want to know what I've discovered?' said Joe finally, and perhaps also to change the subject.

'Joe's been to Los Alamos,' I added, 'and uncovered some amazing truths.'

They did want to know, but Mack was even more intent on following up his and Adam's morning's work. 'We need to send a telegram, communicate with Wolf, give him the good news.' They told us about the names, the telegram, the phone-call, the procedures, carefully steering away from how the information had been extracted.

'Come on, you guys,' I said impatiently, 'we came all the way up to New Mexico to ask Joe to solve something vital for us, and he has. The least you can do is show interest.'

'We've got all the time in the world for that, Tessa,' said Mack.

Joe just said quietly, 'Don't worry; it can wait.' I looked at Adam, I suppose for a decision, but he seemed withdrawn and, at least for the moment, to have yielded the leadership to Mack. Looking back, I think Adam was never quite the same again after the pueblo incident, resigning himself maybe to some personal sense of inevitability. 'Okay,' Joe finally said to Mack, 'there's the phone; it's all yours.'

I said, 'No, it's obvious we mustn't on any account implicate this house, this household, or its occupants.' I looked hard at Mack. 'Remember, *you* said that. Let's at least find a post office to call from.'

'Tell us again the procedure,' said Joe.

'We send Wolf a telegram - here's the address (Mack waved the slip of paper); we leave a phone number and a time. It's as simple as that. Wolf receives it and we're waiting by the phone.'

'What are you going to tell him when he does ring?' asked Joe.

'Mission completed,' said Mack, eager to get going.

'Let's think this out, Mack,' said Joe. 'Wouldn't it be much better to leave him in the dark completely? Keep him waiting? Your mission's only half completed anyway. *He's* the guy you want, not Spectre. He's the instigator.'

'So let's keep him in the frame then.'

'Don't alert your enemy unless you have to,' said Joe.

I knew Joe was right. 'And listen, Mack,' I said, 'what are we going to *do* with Hateley, even supposing we make contact? We've got nothing on him yet.'

'Sure we have. He's the guy who paid Spectre to kill Mr. J. Isn't that enough?'

'You don't know *why* he did. You don't know his reasons, and he'll just deny all knowledge of Spectre.'

Adam at last said, 'Tessa's right, Mack. We only know half. We need to know what's at the back of it all. There's a cover-up going on.'

Our combined arguments prevailed. Mack retreated. Joe said, 'And I guarantee the secret lies in what I discovered today. Have a look, you guys.' He produced a sheet of paper on which he'd written the deciphered code. 'Okay, first of all the names: they're obvious, and we assume that for '*Jackson*', we read '*Jackson Snr*'. It makes sense. Tessa's already filled me in on that assumption.'

'And the anagram?'

'It breaks down into two words: *silent grave*.'

No one said anything for a moment, until - I think it was Adam - said quietly, slowly, 'Are you sure?'

Joe looked up at him. 'I can't find another combination. Certainly not a better one. It's got to be right.'

There was a long silence, all of us trying to interpret those two stark words.

Adam finally said, "*revealing st*' becomes '*silent grave*'. I suppose then, at a stretch, both phrases could be saying the same thing.'

'That's right,' replied Joe quickly. 'It's a clever clue. Both the clue and the solution hint at the same thing.'

'Are you thinking the same as me, Joe?' said Mack.

Joe grinned. 'I expect so. Get digging is what I'm thinking.' The implications were colossal.

After a moment, Adam summed it up. 'So it looks like we've got a body somewhere, in an unmarked grave.'

'I reckon so,' said Joe. 'A body they didn't want anyone to find. Who is '*st*' Adam?'

Adam shook his head. 'Your guess is as good as mine. If we knew that, we'd know everything.'

Joe said, 'Then let's be logical. Go back to first base. Where did this coded message originate? Who wrote it?'

Adam shrugged. 'Once again, I can't be sure.'

'Was it Bill Jackson?'

'I got the note from Bill Jackson, but I doubt he wrote it; it seemed a copy, not the original.' Adam hesitated and then went on, 'He can't have written it or we wouldn't be here right now, getting you to crack it. He couldn't crack it himself, that's the point.'

Joe thought about it for a second. 'That's not entirely true, but I guess it's probable. So let's assume it. Where did *he* get it then? Who gave it to him?'

'I've no idea,' said Adam. 'But I can tell you when Bill Jackson started to change, become depressed, when paranoia set in.'

'When?' said Joe urgently.

'It was that day in Dallas, that Sunday after the assassination. I've just remembered what he said to me.'

'When exactly? What were the circumstances?'

'We were in Dallas, and Ruby had just popped Oswald off. Bill went in to visit a friend somewhere nearby, and I waited in the car. Thirty minutes later he came out and….' Adam stopped mid-flow as if trying desperately to remember something, wrestling with some elusive memory. Finally he shook his head. 'No…it's gone again. I thought I'd got it. Hell!... Anyway, Bill came out through the gate, we drove off, and then he said, *'I think I've just been given a death sentence'.'* Adam hesitated, trying desperately again to wrest some memory from its hiding-place.

'Did he mean the note?' prompted Joe.

'I don't know. I never saw the note until much later. But something had unsettled him. He was heavily depressed that evening. And it was from that point, I know, he started getting ill.'

I said, 'I'm sure it was the assassination. We were all affected.'

'I thought that too at the time, of course. It might have been, but…' he hesitated, 'but it might on the other hand have been something else entirely.'

There was a long silence until Mack broke it. 'Well, you guys, we're beating around the bush. What are we going to do now?'

'You go send your telegram, Mack,' said Adam. 'I know you're desperate to, and anyway, I think it's important we find out if Spectre was a better liar than we thought.'

Joe then said, 'Wait, you guys, before you get carried away. Don't you want to find out first where, if not who, *ST* is? You're not going to believe this.'

'Hell, I'd nearly forgotten,' said Adam.

Joe indicated once more the piece of paper on the table. 14SQC 01210 112221100. Underneath he'd scrawled: 14SQC 0138 4885. 'This is what it looks like when converted back into decimal, remember? We were right, the original was in base 3.'

'For what reason?' said Mack.

Joe grinned. 'Just added security. No other reason. I guess whoever wrote this message wanted to wrap it up real tight. The whole thing is an incredible piece of convolution.'

'More cloak and dagger gibberish,' volunteered Mack. 'So what do those numbers tell us?'

'It's a national grid reference, as I thought. They've got an incredible system down at Los Alamos. They can locate any point in the United States to within an inch.'

'Where is this one then?'

He looked up. 'It's in Texas. Which I suppose is consistent with these guys on the list being Texans.'

'Where in Texas?'

'This is the unbelievable bit. Tessa says you guys are shacked up at Gordonville, by Lake Texoma. This reference pin-points a spot about 3km from Gordonville, on the highway going north towards the lake.'

Mack said 'gee', while I heard Adam mutter, 'This is more than co-incidence.'

Joe grinned and pulled out what looked like a black and white photo. 'The information even comes with a picture, courtesy of the National Laboratory.'

We all bent to look. Adam said, 'How does the reference work exactly?'

'The first bunch of characters - those with the letters - locate a broad area in the US; in this case, the Texoma area. The other two bunches of numbers locate the point precisely.'

'So those fascists in the Pentagon can napalm it,' said Mack.

'Probably,' Joe agreed. 'It works like the way Akens used to try and teach us in Geography: '*along the corridor and up the stairs*'. But you guys don't need to worry about all that; just take this high-altitude photo and there's your 'silent grave'.' We looked closely at the black and white markings. Joe continued, 'Marked with an X to make it even simpler.' He indicated a cross, near what looked like a tree and two other blurry objects. 'You can't go wrong; start digging there.'

'What are those other two little objects, by the tree, Joe?' I asked.

'Probably a couple of rocks. So, you find your two rocks and your tree, and you start digging.' Joe placed his finger on the X.

'In the middle of the night, yeah.' Mack's voice was sceptical, tinged with that sarcasm he used whenever things didn't match up to his precise and logical view of the world. His mind, I think, was still hunting Hateley, not digging in the hard ground for some uncertain remains. *Dispose of Hateley's henchman, dispose of Hateley; problem solved.* I know that's what he was thinking. Joe, more pliable of temperament, just said, smiling, 'Take a flashlight then.'

I had at that moment the impression this business, for him, was finished, that he considered his job done and would be glad if we went. He wanted to be with Darcy and their child; he didn't want to be a part of this whole unreal thing we were embarked on.

Adam said, looking at the photo, 'So, where exactly are we, in the great scale of things? Let's be certain.'

'This picture, this map if you like, is incredibly large scale and detailed,' replied Joe. 'It covers an area of no more than half a kilometre each way.' He indicated two prominent marks near a clear strip indicating a road. 'These two mound-looking objects are 'Noel Cemetery', probably the site an old local burial ground. You've probably passed them hundreds of times as you drive to the Lake.'

'I remember seeing them,' said Adam, glancing at me for confirmation.

'Yeah,' said Joe, 'they stand out. You couldn't miss them.'

'Probably contains the remains of a guy called 'Noel',' said Mack.

'That and others,' said Joe. 'But don't start digging there; you'll be at it all night, digging up bona fide corpses.'

'Great,' interjected Mack. Joe said, 'You guys are looking for an unmarked, unknown grave. Walk approximately 200m north, north east from Noel's. There won't be a mound there.'

'No, but, as you say, there'll be a tree and some rocks at least,' said Adam. 'I wonder why they didn't choose a spot in open ground; somewhere far less easy to locate.'

'Wanted to make *your* life more simple,' said Joe, grinning. 'Why else?'

'I think, it's because, like us, they wanted to be able to find the place easily themselves,' I said. 'And perhaps dig the remains up in a hurry.'

'That's why you guys don't want to give them the chance.' Joe handed the picture over. 'Don't lose this you guys. It's your route to an easy life, and I could only squeeze one copy out of Los Alamos. You'd better head off and start digging.'

We had what we'd come for; there was no reason to stay any longer. We'd be back in Texas by nightfall. We'd already wasted a lot of Joe's time, and we needed to move fast. Mack however was still set on contacting the Wolf; the challenge was too much for him to resist. So we made what was, I suppose, our first mistake.

'There's no point doing it up here, Mack,' I said. 'There'll be a delay of at least 24 hours, while Hateley receives the telegram.'

And Adam added, 'Why not send the telegram when we get back, Mack? Find a phone-box and a contact number in Gordonville straightaway.' Mack agreed reluctantly.

'What are you going to tell him when he rings?' asked Joe, a hint of scepticism in his voice. I remembered how, back at Hillcrest, Mack and Joe had often crossed swords whenever Mack's petulance and Joe's common-sense had been at odds.

'Tell the little shit-head his life in the fast lane is coming to an end.'

'That's not going to help anything, Mack.'

'Why not?'

'It's bound to alert him that something's not as it should be. He presumably knows your location at Gordonville. He'll send someone else out to watch you and you're back to square one.'

'Okay, then let's find somewhere else to live,' said Mack.

Joe broke the silence that followed that remark, and said abruptly, 'I wash my hands of the business. I wish you guys luck. I've got a wife and kid to support - soon to be another, I think.' We congratulated him and Darcy; he grinned in that enigmatic way I remembered so well. 'If things were different, if things were even like they were two years ago, I might be tempted to join you. But I'm afraid Hillcrest isn't what it used to be. From all reports.'

How do you mean Joe?' I said, a note of concern in my voice.

He shrugged his shoulders. 'It's just rumour, Tess. But I've heard the place has become a kind of cult.'

My heart sank. 'A cult? It can't have changed that much. Not in just a couple of years.'

Joe seemed reluctant to discuss it further. 'As I said, merely rumour. But it doesn't take long for things like that to happen, to take root.'

The others had been silently listening. Now Adam said, 'It was kind of going that way, Tess, even when we were there.' I glanced at him, puzzled. He went on, 'Look at the disgraceful way Mr J was ejected. And even Joe and Darce here. That complete farcical cover-up.'

Joe said, 'I hear it's worse now, much worse.'

We all stood dismayed. I said, 'How exactly then?' Joe shook his head. 'Not much teaching goes on apparently. Not much of anything we'd recognise. Open sex on campus; phoney religious gatherings, abuse of leadership, that sort of weird stuff.'

I said, 'I just can't believe it.'

There was shocked silence for a minute in the room and Joe added, 'I can't afford to risk it. I guess I'm in the rat-race now, willy-nilly.'

'Don't use that ridiculous word, Joe,' said Darcy, grasping his arm.

'I picked it up from the limeys, I think. A legacy from Hillcrest.'

'Well you're no longer at Hillcrest,' she drawled 'so you don't need to speak like them. And you're not in any rat-race either, Joe Verard; you're destined for a great career. Why in heaven's name d'you think I married you?'

'You married me,' said Joe, looking at us but talking to Darcy, 'because you got pregnant.'

'Sure as hell doesn't mean I had to marry you,' said Darcy defiantly.

We drove off, leaving them standing there on the sidewalk. But I thought of Joe as we headed south that afternoon. Darcy was right, about the career, and I knew it. Two years ago, Joe appeared to have screwed up his life, drummed out of high-school and rejected by those who should have known better - those on our list in fact, those who, it appears, had many wayward, dark stories to tell about their own youths, stories we were hopefully going to find out about. And as for Joe, he'd put it all back together again, while we, clutching at straws, set off in pursuit of madmen, risking our lives on a whim. I envied him, but said nothing. In my heart though I'd begun to feel very apprehensive about this whole business.

And something else too that I'd told no one about: I'd missed my period twice now.

PART II

THE COURT OF ELSINORE

"I will work him
To an exploit now ripe in my device,
Under the which he shall not choose but fall."

Bridgeport, Connecticut, Fall 1967

At about the time of our triumphant return from Santa Fe and those first inklings of my pregnancy, I received a letter from my brother, sent *poste restante* to Gordonville; it was a blistering letter, full of anger and hate, an attack on both me and the secret child inside me, and dispelling any maternal sensations of joy I might have been having.

I picked the letter up at Gordonville, where it had finally been sent on by my mother, after its long journey via London and Connecticut. George himself was obviously unaware of all my comings and goings and certainly of my current address; communication on even the most superficial level was not in my brother's nature, although he clearly felt within his rights to interfere in family matters of a much more personal and significant kind.

I was clearly pregnant and was going to have Adam's child, although how this got back to George I never did find out, but can only suppose, in the light of subsequent events, it was via Charlene and Slater. The information might in fact even have originated from Hateley himself, knowing the many sensitive tendrils he could put out into the most innocent and unexpected corners; George mentions Hateley briefly too in the letter, and the most probable explanation for all of this is that he, Charlene, Slater and Hateley met together sometime in August '67 (my brother was already working at that time as a medical intern at the Denber local hospital), and hatched their dire scenario. It's impossible to discount George's full complicity in the plot, such was his egotism and self-righteous attitude towards the world and the people in it.

His vicious attack contained in the letter, on me personally, was deeply hurtful: '*I always knew you'd get yourself into trouble one day, Tessa…I can only find one word to describe your behaviour; that word is 'sluttish'…that I should have had the misfortune to be saddled with a sluttish sister…';* however the highlight of the letter, the most telling part, was the prophetic warning: *'…I will not be able to account for my actions if I'm ever to come face to face with that cowardly good-for-nothing, Riley'.* What irony lay in those words! It's clear he must have known he would, before long, indeed come 'face to face' with Adam, (the trap was almost certainly sprung by the time of the letter); even George though can't have imagined the bizarre role he would play in that encounter.

'Yes, I am indeed to have a baby, the child of someone I love, and considering your apparent disdain for the entire human race, your sister included, you would do best to keep your opinions to yourself and mind your own business'. This is what I angrily wrote back to my brother, adding that such people as he was, were not what was right with the world, but rather what was wrong with it: those self-seeking, cold, hostile, heartless people, inhabitants merely, and unable to realise that other people, fellow-humans, are as important a part of life as money and the dubious trappings of success, which he so single-mindedly sought. How could he choose such a naturally charitable profession when it was clear to all - even surely to himself - that his one concern in life was to remain uninvolved? '*Do you remember, George, how you once told us you wouldn't reach adulthood until you were forty? I secretly admired you at the time, but it's plain to see in hindsight that those words*

were mere self-deception on your part; you will never be adult (I angrily underlined it) until you stop hating others and begin to feel some sort of responsibility towards them'.

My god, how much we hated each other at this juncture. Nor now can I see any way to forgive him, any reconciliation, as events have, by now, moved inexorably towards their dreadful denouement….

Uncovering

On the route back from Santa Fe, stuck in the car together, we debated our predicament. Should we dig, should we pay a visit to San Antonio and Mrs. Jackson Snr, or should we instantly contact Hateley? To me, the first course of action was the obvious one; things, according to the coded message, pointed to some very bad business, but it was only a message. We had to know for sure. Mack wanted to contact Hateley though straightaway.

'If we don't contact him, he's bound to get suspicious, come looking for us himself.'

'If we do contact him,' said Adam, 'he's bound to get suspicious too. Why don't we just wait; let him stew in his own juice, wait for a telegram from Mongrel that never arrives, while we unearth some more vital evidence.'

'If it's there,' said Mack.

But, in spite of his thirst for a showdown with Hateley, we managed to persuade him to be patient. Thinking about it at the time, I wondered, in fact, if Mack's desire to avenge Mr. Jackson's murder was stronger even than mine or Adam's.

'I think it's definitely there, Mack,' I said, 'whatever it is, and might reveal some even dirtier business than what we already know.'

Mack shrugged. 'Maybe. I've got an open mind.'

Back at Texoma next day, we acted fast. Decisions now made, we were in a hurry to '*reveal st*'. I think all of us knew it was the key to everything and that our mission was reaching a culmination. We would dig that same evening.

Mack went off to Wal-Mart to fetch equipment, while Adam and I found new accommodation, in Sherman. It was a 'Fall let'. Temporary only.

'Suits us fine,' we told the real estate agent. What we didn't tell her was that, if by the end of the Fall we hadn't completed our mission, we were either dead or had abandoned what had proved an impossible task. The new accommodation was a small house on Crockett St, near the junction with Lamar, and not far from the main square. In the heart of downtown Sherman. We wouldn't attract attention there and would disappear off Hateley's radar once again, even supposing he didn't already believe us despatched at the hands of his invincible henchman.

We had a while to wait before we were due to meet Mack. I went into the town library to do some digging (of another kind), while Adam waited for Mack at the rendezvous. I wanted to see what I could find out about those other members on our list of seven: *Hateley, Faulkner, Philips, Foreman, Miller, McDiarmid, Jackson.* I quickly and speculatively looked up Philips, Miller and McDiarmid in the local '*Who's Who*'. Amazingly, all three were listed (they were clearly wealthy men; so why wouldn't they be?). The entry under *Harvey.J.Philips* was quite short: *Born 1911 in Argyle, Denber County; attended Harvard Law School; founded the Philips law practice in Dallas in 1942; member of the board on numerous local charities; active in the Rotarians; served in the National Guard during World War II; interests include philately and duck-hunting.*

William.T.Miller: *Born 1908 in Clarendon, Texas; served briefly in the Dallas Police Department before being elected the youngest ever Sheriff of Denber County at the age of 30; saw active service in Europe in 1944 with the 141st US Infantry Regiment (First Texas); retired in 1950 to run the family ranch in Clarendon; member of the Board of Governors at the Hillcrest School, Denber, from where his two children have recently been graduated.* (I already preferred the sound of Miller to Philips. What was his part on this dubious list?).

I finally found McDiarmid. His listing was brief: *Born in Aubrey, Denber County in 1915; only son of local landowner, Lawrence.S.McDiarmid; active in state politics and member of the*

Nixon team in the 1960 presidential election. Little else of importance about him in '*Who's Who*', so I hurriedly looked through past copies of the Denber Record Chronicle, searching for a mention of him, some reference around Christmas 1963. And there suddenly it was: an entry in the 'DRC' of January 15th, 1964 under '***Mysterious disappearance of son of local landowner***': '*... disappearance of James.M.McDiarmid while holidaying in western New Mexico in late December of last year....*' Triumph. I didn't need to read further. He almost certainly died at the hands of William Jackson Jnr or else the 'Mongrel' (as Adam and Mack called him). We still didn't know how or why and probably never would.

As for the remaining members on our list, I didn't bother to look up their provenance. We knew them already: Hateley (Board of Governors), Faulkner (local landowner and prolific benefactor of the Hillcrest School), Foreman (Chairman of the Board), William Jackson Snr (hopefully his widow would tell us a whole lot more about him and his role on this list). I took copies of all that I'd found and returned, elated, to our rendezvous, where Mack and Adam waited, surrounded by shovels and picks.

'Triumph!'

'Where the hell have you been, Tessa?'

'Don't worry, guys. Sorry to keep you waiting; it was in a good cause.' I brandished my copies. 'Let's go.' All in all, I remember it - this whole trip to Sherman - as a joyous, positive, constructive interlude before the gruesome business that awaited us.

'And, by the way,' I said, 'this tranquil, respectable little town where we've just rented lodgings was once not so tranquil: a hundred years ago a favourite watering-hole of Jesse James and his gang, one of the hottest spots in the Wild West, riots, you name it. I looked it up; a very rotten reputation indeed.'

Adam roared with laughter as we drove back towards Gordonville. 'Nothing's changed then really. For 'Jesse James and his gang', read 'Charlie Hateley and *his* gang'.'

'Yeah,' said Mack 'maybe we can entice them sometime to come and drink at our watering-hole.'

*****

And there at last we were, at the end of the final week of August, setting out like thieves in the night, armed with picks and shovels, to dig into the hard ground for the remains of who? We didn't know who, just the remains of '*st*'. It was a dark night, no moon.

'Remember,' said Adam, taking charge (as if this one, this particular task of the mission, was dearer to him than any other) 'we don't want anyone, not anyone, to see us, or we're all lost: end of mission, perhaps even the end of us.'

We reached the mounds denoting Noel's Cemetery, off to the right, some twenty yards away from the road: two quite large and unusual hillocks covered in grass.

'Park the car up a further half-a-mile. Just in case some nosey cop drives this way.' It was already past midnight. Unlikely.

'Mr. R, we can't trudge back with all this gear,' said Mack.

'Leave it here by the mounds then.'

'Why don't I just wait here for you guys to come back?' said Mack.

'No, we don't want to split up.'

We left the sack full of Mack's gear by the edge of the left-hand mound, out of sight and totally in darkness (you'd have needed a torch to spot it even from two or three yards away), took the torches (one each), drove on and found a spot to park the car three quarters of a mile up the road. And we trudged back.

'Remember,' said Adam, 'if anyone sees us and stops, then no, we don't want a lift and, yes, we got stuck at the lake, car out of gas, heading back to Gordonville, enjoying the walk.'

No one saw us. No cars around at this time. We picked up the sack and looked north east. We shone the torches. Typical of the low scrubland that surrounded the lake, ahead of us lay an area of quite dense foliage, a host of little trees dotted around, and, among them, bushes, some of them intertwining, clinging to the hard, stony soil beneath the sand.

'Christ,' said Mack. 'Hope we're going to find this little baby. Isn't it a couple of trees we're looking for?'

'Yes,' said Adam, shining the torch onto the map, 'but we're looking for two distinct rocks as well. All we can do is make our way in the right direction. It's definitely north, north-east from the alignment of the road, which at this point is exactly due north.'

Keeping the road in sight for as long as possible, we set off, stumbling from time to time (even falling).

'What's the distance again?' called Mack.

'200 metres.'

'I'm going to count them then.' And he did.

'Don't forget,' called Adam, 'we're hardly going straight.'

'It'll be a fair approximation though,' I said, hoping to encourage the other two.

The road had disappeared. We were lost in amongst this scrub. All we could do, flashlight beams fastened on the ground, was head in what we assumed was the right direction. Mack, carrying the load, stumbled and fell again, cursed silently and said, 'Not a bad spot this for a piece of gruesome night-work.' He picked himself up and continued counting: 150, 151, 152....I was thinking: the unlikeliest spot in all the world for a grave and a body. It had also occurred to me that digging into this ground after months of no rain would be horribly difficult. I said nothing, but laboured on, following Mack, who in turn was following Adam. '...193, 194, 195....' A car came by, heading back from the direction of the lake.

'Douse the lights,' hissed Adam. We were plunged into complete darkness, standing stock still, scarcely daring to breathe. The car passed us, the headlights disappearing away off to our left. 'A lovers' tryst,' Adam murmured.

'...207, 208, 209....' Mack's voice was registering increasing signs of panic. Is there a more awful sensation in life than the feeling of utter desperation and powerlessness that accompanies a failed mission? We weren't going to succeed. We'd lost our way. '...220, 221, 222, 223....'

And then up front came a cry out of the darkness. 'I think I've got it.' Adam was shining his torch over to the right, where the beam revealed a sort of clearing, and distinctly two quite large, adjacent rocks and, four or so yards to the right of them, a larger than usual fir tree. Yes.

We staggered into the clearing and Mack flung down his load, joyfully exclaiming, 'Thank god for Verard. We owe that guy a lot!'

It was flat, sandy soil, without any trace of a rise in the ground. Adam studied the map for a moment, and went and stood midway (pacing it out) between the tree and the right-hand rock. 'X marks the spot.' Where he stood gave no sign of being different from anywhere else in the clearing. 'We'll just have to trust Joe's navigational skills, and get digging.'

We took it in turns to labour at that ground, sandy at first, but increasingly hard. We hurled the point of the pick-axes at it as if each blow was dealing a *coup de grace* to some hated being. We scraped the soil away and dug in with the shovels, all of us working now, from different sides. After an hour the ground began to give slightly as if the lake's natural moisture had penetrated it over the years. We'd made a six-by-six foot hole, no deeper than two feet. Across the hole, we looked silently at each other, probably all thinking the same thing, as, first, frustration, then doubt, came licking at our throats: If we found nothing here, the coded message came to nothing, Bill's desperate letter signified nothing, everything spelled nothing. We had to find something beyond just sand and damp mud. We yearned for a body.

Another twenty minutes passed and I know in my heart I'd given up. Adam and Mack shone their flashlights into the hole.

'We're wasting our time, Mr. R.' Mack flung the point of his shovel into the earth, while Adam, bewildered, looked across at us from the other side of the hole. 'There's gotta be something.' And I said (but not meaning it), 'Graves can go *down* six feet as well.' (Did any of us really believe this could be more than just a shallow grave?). And Mack's shovel, instead of holding fast in the soil, striking something and falling flat on the ground.

Ten seconds. Ten impossibly expectant moments, before Adam was kneeling inside the grave and, with enormous care, like an archaeologist exposing a new sarcophagus, was brushing away the soil with his fingers, where the tip of Mack's shovel had gone in, while we focused our torches on the vital spot. For a moment, mole-like, his fingers delved into the soil; then he looked up and said, 'It's here.'

A skull, a skeleton. Well-formed (if you can say such a thing of a skeleton), well preserved. Here, in this unlikely spot, it had lain, just deep enough to escape the ravages of possum and badgers, for, how long? Science would be able to tell; criminal pathologists were becoming expert these days: they could pin-point age, sex, race even.

'The shovel hit it,' exclaimed Adam.

Mack seemed not to hear. 'Do we get the cops in, Mr. R?'

'For chrissakes, Mack, no, we don't!' He was adamant. 'A body in an unmarked grave: newsmen, cameramen, lawyers, fingers pointing at us, Hateley alerted. No, this is our trump card; we, and no one else, know of the existence of this grave.'

'Except those who made it,' said Mack, and laughed excitedly.

'Yeah,' replied Adam, 'correct. They're on the other side of the law though.' He came back out of the grave, and said firmly, 'We cover it up again, okay? Carefully.' Silence. Just the usual night noises, the frogs, the rustle of a possum or a skunk maybe, stopping to observe this unlikely scene. Adam added, 'We keep it for a rainy day.'

I said, 'Yes, and also I think we should document all this, date it - get the date from the top of a newspaper or something - and set the record straight on paper. Put it in a safe-box. Just in case.'

'Send it to a newspaper,' added Mack. 'Great idea.'

'Meanwhile, let's get out of here quick,' said Adam. 'Let's put the earth back as untouched as it was before.' Adam and Mack started shovelling.

'Poor skeleton. Bye bye,' Mack said, as the earth plumped gradually back into the hole. Then after a second he added, 'Hey, wait a minute.' He jumped from the edge of the grave down into the soft earth. Adam stopped shovelling. The beam of my torch played on the disappearing bones in the earth. 'Look at this, you guys,' Mack called. 'Tessa, shine your torch exactly where my finger is; here, on the skull.' I did. 'Look,' he went on, 'it's been hit, bashed in, mincemeat. I'm amazed we didn't notice before.' We looked. He was right: the back of the skull was badly indented. 'Dirty work indeed. I hope *we* didn't do that.'

'No,' Adam said, 'the shovel can't have done all that; that looks like some massive blow.'

'Sweet skeleton,' Mack said, transferring his gaze now to the fragile slivers of bone that made up the left forearm. 'Tess, shine here.' With one deft movement, as I transferred the beam, he broke off a finger bone and held it up for us to see. 'A memento.' Where he knelt, he pushed clumps of earth over the skeleton as best he could. 'Thanks, whoever you are.' He climbed out of the grave again. 'Who is it, you guys? We owe him, or her, a lot.'

'It's '*st*'', said Adam. 'Esther. I'm inclined to think our friend is female. The bones are small and the whole figure short.'

We finished covering it up, patting it down till it was level again. Mack ran a small branch backwards and forwards across it, trying to eradicate any prints. As I stood watching, Adam looked at me and said, 'Wyoming folklore.'

'You guys don't need to be so cynical,' called Mack. 'I'm doing you a favour.'

'The rain'll do that anyway, I suspect,' said Adam. 'Let's go.' We took a last look at our work. 'Not so 'silent' now,' said Mack, and I said, 'When this business is all over, I'm coming back to give this grave a proper memorial.'

Adam said, stumbling through the bushes back to the road, 'I expect whoever wrote that note will see to that anyway in time.'

'Then it wasn't Mr. J?' It came out as a question.

'No, I don't think so; he got it from someone else and handed it on to us.' Those words must have triggered something in his mind because, all at once, at the edge of the road, he was leaping around, shovel in hand, shouting, 'Christ! For heaven's sake, you guys. I think I've got it. I think I've remembered the thing.' We waited silently. He continued, calmer now, working it out. 'There was someone at the gate. That day. Someone saying goodbye to Bill hastily.'

'*What* day, Mr. R?'

'The day I went down to Dallas with Bill. Doomsday. The day Ruby killed Oswald.'

'Sunday,' I said.

'Yes, Sunday, and Bill went in to see a friend….' He hesitated, recalling it. 'After a while he came out, and there was someone with him at the gate.'

'Who, Adam?' I said. 'Did you get a good look?'

'No, I was distracted anyway. By Spectre's presence.'

'Christ!' said Mack impatiently, half to himself, while Adam continued, visualising the moment, willing it to re-appear. 'The friend was a black man. Yes, young. Bill's age. I recall that. And then he half waved and shut the gate, and Bill was back beside me in the car, and we were worrying about Spectre all over again.'

'Who was this friend, Adam?' I said.

'I don't know.' Adam was still in a state of excitement.

'*Where* was it then?'

'I don't really know that either. We were in a Dallas suburb; somewhere not far from the Dallas courthouse. South Dallas perhaps.'

'Would you be able to find your way there again?' My questions were urgent. Instinctively I was sure this was the key.

'I doubt it. Maybe.' He hesitated, and then said, 'But I'm fairly sure now Bill received the message from that guy.'

As we drove back to Gordonville - 3 o'clock in the morning - Adam calmed down. He said, 'I'm sorry, you guys. It was such a fleeting glimpse. But suddenly, back there (he indicated behind us in the darkness), it all linked up.'

'Must have been Esther giving us a parting word,' said Mack, and we all laughed, and Adam said, 'You're probably righter than you think.'

Mack replied, 'Hum hah, Mr. R and all his ghosts and spirits.'

The rest of the short journey passed in silence. We were tired.

*****

Annie Avenue was a quiet street in the Olmos Park area of San Antonio, tucked in among a huddle of tree-lined suburban avenues bordering the park and the golf courses. It was the kind of place a well-to-do widow might choose to live out her days, in peace.

Peace. Far from it. As we glided up the wide street looking for No.333, the notion even made me smile. Mack had proposed that morning - the day following the dig - we pay Bill Jackson's mother a 'formal' visit, posing as FBI agents. 'I've already got the necessaries.' He produced little badges and photos to be inserted into wallets.

Adam and I had looked astounded at the merchandise. 'Where the hell did you get all this gear, Mack?'

'Wal-Mart, when I was buying the shovels. Thought it'd be a good idea.' There was a sense of achievement, almost pride, in his voice.

'Why?'

'The old lady won't hold anything back when confronted with officers of the law.'

Adam and I were clearly both thinking the opposite. 'D'you really believe Bill's widow is more likely to deliver the goods to FBI agents than to former students of her dead son?'

Mack hesitated. 'Just thought we might get more out of her. Anyway, what in hell's name is it we want to get out of the old biddy? Seems a long way to go.'

Adam didn't answer his question, but just said, 'Cops'll scare the wits out of her. She's an old lady for heaven's sake, Mack.'

And I added (cattily, I admit), 'Why don't you focus on the bodyguard role, Mack, and leave the thinking to me and Adam?'

At that moment - and perhaps prompted by my hostile remark - Adam did something very odd and unexpected. He put his arm gently round Mack's shoulder and said, 'Listen, my partner in crime, my Buddy, I already owe you a million dollars in back pay; I'll never make good that debt, but I know you won't ask for it either.' As he tightened his hold round Mack's shoulder, he added, 'What you've done for us has been invaluable. Don't think I don't know. If ever I've needed help and friendship, it's been in these past few days, and you've given both.'

It was almost touching, almost theatrical in its effect. The two of them standing there, linked, seeming to pose for a photo. A bond, I realised, had been established up on that cliff-top in New Mexico, that could never be broken, never be shared by anyone else: they'd risked their lives together, each of them relying blindly on the other. No, I was not a part of that fellowship.

I apologised to Mack for my remark and went off to make a phone-call to Margaret Jackson while, behind me, I heard Mack say (kindly, humorously), 'Okay, Tessa, you second-generation, limey, brown-nose teacher's pet, let's see what brilliant ideas you can come up with today.'

'Students of Bill?' said the frail voice down the other end of the line. 'Why sure; I'd love you to pay a visit. Students of my son, Bill!' She repeated the words as if scarcely able to believe this resurrection. 'When would you like to visit?'

'How about this afternoon, Mrs. Jackson? By chance we're in San Antonio this afternoon.'

Hesitation down the line, the uncertainty of an old person caught napping, not having everything in place, ship-shape. Then the voice said, 'Do you have the address? Did Bill give it to you?'

I wondered if the question sounded as strange to her as it did to me. 'No, Mrs. Jackson, can you give it to me?'

I emerged from the call-box thinking that perhaps Mack this morning had inadvertently stumbled upon the most appropriate way to visit this woman, this wife who'd lost her husband, this mother who'd lost her son, both in the space of six short months: *let's make this formal, you guys; pose as FBI agents*. Formal, official, unemotional, sparing her the ghosts that were bound to arise from any visit by friends or acquaintances. There were, for instance, matters that were certain to be emotive: the questionable death of her husband for one. FBI agents would get over that problem much more simply: '*We're treating your husband's death as homicide, Mrs. Jackson*'. I dreaded the coming visit.

Before setting off for San Antonio, we'd moved our stuff from Gordonville to our new place at Sherman, and I'd made a start on a written testimony of our strange mission. If, now, while still in control of events, we set down in detail all the unusual circumstances surrounding the affair, we'd be much more likely to be believed if things started to go wrong.

Mack had said, 'We should post the narrative to two or three significant bodies, as well as to Joe.' With his usual sense of the dramatic, he added, 'Mark it: TO BE OPENED IN THE EVENT OF THE DEATH OF ONE OR MORE OF THE SIGNEES. '

I'd shuddered. 'Try not to be too dramatic, Mack.'

Adam, more concerned with the details, wanted me to skim over any references to the circumstances surrounding Spectre's disappearance. 'You never know if that'll come back to haunt us.'

'But I don't know the circumstances anyway,' I said.

'Just as well, then; what you don't know, you can't report.'

'But I'll have to say *something*.'

'Make it up, Tessa; you always had a vivid imagination.'

And so we'd set off for San Antonio. The woman who opened the door to 333 was just as I'd imagined: small, somewhat frail, well-dressed, carefully turned out, quaint almost, but clearly determined to keep up appearances. We stood there on the doorstep like the Three Stooges, clumsy and uncomfortable, even less presentable than FBI agents with phoney badges.

'Well, you must be Bill's students. How nice of you to visit. You'all come right in.' She turned to me. 'And you must be the young lady who phoned me. You sounded like a thousand miles away. I don't get a lot of phone-calls these days.'

'Yes, that's right, Mrs. Jackson; we've come for....' But what *had* we come for? To inform her that, contrary to popular belief, her son had been cut down in his prime on the orders of a fanatic with some murderous secret? That this same person had also had her husband despatched for the same reasons? She probably wouldn't have believed it. We had to be more subtle than that. Adam must have noticed my hesitation, because he interrupted me. 'We've come for some information, Mrs. Jackson, which we think you can provide. I have to come clean; this isn't entirely an informal visit.'

And Margaret Jackson, from the kitchen, where she'd gone to prepare some coffee, called, 'I *had* kind of suspected something like that, my dears. Young folk like yourselves don't just visit old ladies.' Then she added after a pause, 'Not unless, that is, they want her money!'

'No, we don't want your money, Mrs. Jackson. You can rest assured of that.' Adam looked at us and whispered, 'Leave this to me, you guys.'

She came back in with a tray of coffee and placed it on the side-table. It was Bill, her son, she wanted to talk about. 'So what did you'all study under Bill?'

Adam explained. 'Mack and Tessa here studied English literature. I didn't study anything; I was a teacher at Hillcrest, together with Bill.'

Her eyes lit up. 'So you were a colleague of my son's.'

Adam nodded. 'Colleague and friend. He was a wonderful teacher, Mrs. Jackson.' Adam placed great emphasis on the remark.

'Everybody said so. He was doing real well there.' There was a lull; the topic seemed to be exhausted and drifting towards areas she might well have wished to avoid. But then she said, 'I never could understand why things began to go wrong. If Bill Snr had been around, he'd have surely intervened in that ghastly business, when they drummed Bill out, just like that. Bill....'

She wanted to continue, but Adam leaned towards her and interrupted her. 'Margaret, Bill was totally innocent of any charges. We know that. You have to believe us.'

With the light for a moment gone out of her eyes, she said, 'I'd like to believe you.'

And then it was all coming out, the nub of the matter. Adam said, 'Margaret, we've made a number of enquiries over the past few months; enquiries in high places. We're convinced your son did not commit suicide; we think he was murdered.'

Hesitation. She didn't seem so much shocked as numbed. So much reflexion and heartache had dulled the pain in the interim. She said quietly, 'I've sometimes wondered about that myself, you know. It wasn't like Bill to do a thing like that.'

Adam said, 'It wasn't like him at all; we agree.'

But she was still out there, searching desperately for other possibilities, trying to comprehend. 'That impetuous wife of his, all those hostile people at the Hillcrest School.' And then she asked us the vital question, us who already knew the answer. 'Murdered by who?'

Adam waited before replying; he needed to present the evidence carefully. I saw him take our message - that slip of paper with the code - out of his pocket, but instead of handing it to her, he asked, 'D'you know someone called Charles Hateley?'

The question produced a sort of explosion in her. 'Charles Hateley! Sure I know him. I know too it was he at the back of all those allegations against Bill at Hillcrest. Firing him out of hand; what was he thinking....'

Adam didn't let her finish. His tone was urgent. 'Did your husband know him maybe?'

Her mouth split into a bitter smile. 'Charlie Hateley - the 'Fox' we jokingly used to call him, because he looked so like one - sure we knew him; he's been in and out of our lives for as long as I can recall.'

Almost as an afterthought, she added, 'Why might he have done such a thing? Such betrayal!'

'We think he has a secret and that Bill knew it.' Allowing briefly for this news to sink in, Adam handed her the slip of paper. 'Margaret, this is important. Can you tell us why your husband's name should appear, together with all those others, on that list?'

She studied it for a minute and handed it back. 'Sure. Partners in crime, I'd say; ghosts from the bad old days. Bill Snr grew up together with all those fellows: Jimmy McDiarmid, Harvey Philips…Charlie Hateley….'

She was reminiscing. Adam interrupted her. 'What bad old days, Margaret?'

'Oh, nothing really. You know what young folks are like. When my husband was younger. They were all really Denber people, you see, from there and thereabouts. It was before he even met me.'

There was a silence in the room; just the clock ticking. At last, Adam said, 'What was?'

Mrs. Jackson seemed to come back from miles away. 'They were just wild, that's all.' She paused before continuing, 'And then suddenly it all stopped. Bill Snr and I got married quite late, you see.' Once more she hesitated, as if this were the explanation for everything.

'When was that?'

'Let me see…yes, '36. 1936. Shocking I shouldn't remember the year I got married. The economy was starting to pick up; Bill was earning.'

'Margaret, did your husband stop mixing with these other people, these youthful friends of his (he indicated the list again) immediately you got married?' Adam gave me the impression he already knew the answers, and was desperate for evidence, for facts confirming them. It was almost exciting watching him.

'Let me see,' replied Margaret. 'No, it was perhaps a couple of years after that that the partying stopped. Like someone turned the tap off. Those fellows just didn't come visiting anymore; Bill dropped them, like a stone - or they him.' After a second, she added, 'He was occupied anyway at that time. Earning money, business affairs. And Bill Jnr was already on the way.'

'Did he never mix with those people after that time?' Adam's question was direct, specific, insistent, like a terrier sniffing a rabbit.

'I wouldn't exactly say that. The partying stopped, that's all. Charles Hateley continued to visit infrequently, even after Bill was born, but something had gotten in the way; they'd fallen out, I guess, over something. Bill never mentioned what; he just never spoke about it, that's all.'

We'd reached an impasse. The 'why' of the matter refused to budge from its hiding-place. What had happened to cause that sudden rift? We were still no closer to understanding the mystery linking all those names together, and Margaret Jackson seemed unlikely to be able to tell us. The clock ticked, we drank another coffee, Mack began to lose patience and shuffle his feet. Adam finally got up. 'It's been real nice visiting with you, Margaret; what you've been able to tell us about Bill and your husband has been very helpful.'

She shook her head. 'I wish I could have told you more.' Her face momentarily lit up, a glimpse of sunlight breaking through on a cloudy day. 'But if you need me to testify, you can count on me. I long for the opportunity to clear Bill's name.'

'It won't come to that, Margaret,' said Mack quite suddenly, clearly overcome with frustration and unable to conceal it in his voice. 'We just don't have enough evidence.'

The sun disappeared again behind the mass of clouds. 'You kids have worked so hard. I only wish I could have shed some light.' She was accompanying us towards the door.

And all at once I saw it. On the sideboard, a family photo, clearly taken in happier times: she, Bill Snr, (both smiling broadly), three young children standing in front, two boys and a girl, one of the boys easily identifiable as our former teacher, the other boy, next to Bill, taller, older, negro. I edged closer, anxious to avoid arousing any more unnecessary memories in Margaret, but needing to take a closer look. What I saw compelled me spontaneously to pick the photo up, frame and all. I held it out to Margaret.

'Your children are lovely.' I indicated the young Bill. 'That's Bill, isn't it?'

'That's Bill,' she repeated smiling. 'That's Juliet, his sister.'

I didn't give her a chance to finish. I asked, 'Who's the little black boy?'

'That's young Tommy. He grew up with us in the family. Bill Snr just brought him home one evening. He was orphaned; seems he'd lost both his parents.' She reflected for a moment. 'Both Bills loved that boy. I can scarcely bear to look at that photo; Tommy was like another son.'

Adam could scarcely now conceal his excitement. 'When did Tommy first arrive. Margaret? Can you put a year on it?'

'It was the time we've just been talking about, soon after Bill was born. I'd say '38. Sam was about six at the time.'

'Who's Sam?'

'Sam is Tommy. Sam Toms. The little black boy in the photo. We used to call him Tommy, or Sammy. Either would do. He'd jump and respond whichever name we used.'

She'd retreated once more into her day-dreams. Adam however was insistent. 'What had happened to his own parents?'

Margaret shrugged. 'I guess they'd just died.'

'What, both at the same time?'

'I guess. Bill Snr never talked about it. Just insisted we must take Sammy in; bring him up like ours. So the two boys just grew up, inseparable; like two peas in a pod.'

'Didn't Sammy himself ever talk about his parents?'

'Not that I can recall.'

'So you never knew their names.'

She shook her head. 'No, he never mentioned them.' Then after a few moments she added, 'But hold on a moment; I'm forgetting. There *was* just the once. It was when he first came to us, he sometimes used to say (she hesitated, thinking hard), yes, that's it, he used to say, '*Sadie only asleep*'. He said that on several occasions and we took no notice - thought it was just kid's imagination - until one day I said, '*Who's Sadie, Sammie?*' and he looked at me, big brown eyes. '*Mamie, Sadie*'.' Margaret reflected for a moment. 'Yes, that's right: '*Mamie, Sadie*'. He never mentioned her again after that time; it was as if the mention of those two words had erased her from his memory altogether.'

Adam and I looked at each other, thunderstruck. It felt as if the building was about to fall; the last link in the long chain had eased effortlessly into place. Adam said quietly to me, 'Sadie. Sadie Toms. '*st*'.' Then, in a moment, he was back talking to Margaret Jackson. 'And whatever happened to Sammy?'

'He turned out to be a real smart boy. We put him through college. He graduated in Math I think.'

'Where?'

'NTSU.'

'Where is he now, Margaret? Is he still in the locality?'

'I guess so; I sort of lost touch with him when he left home, and when my two Bills died; there was so much going on, you understand.' Adam murmured, 'Of course we do' and took her hand. She continued, 'I think he was doing a post-graduate at SMU. The last I heard, he was living in a house somewhere in Dallas.'

'Do you know where in Dallas, Margaret?'

She shook her head. 'I'm real sorry; I sure don't. All I can remember is that Bill used to visit him when he was doing his political stuff. They weren't so far apart politically, you know.'

Preparing to leave, Adam hugged her and gave her the obligatory kiss on the cheek. 'Don't worry about it; you've been more helpful than you can imagine, Margaret. None of us can begin to tell you how sorry we are about your two Bills. We loved your son and it seems like we'd have loved your husband too. But we'll put matters right, believe me.'

'You're very kind. All of you,' she said. And we left her standing in the doorway, smiling weakly, alone with her memories.

When we got back in the car, Mack vented his frustration. 'What was that guy, Sam, doing writing all that gobbledygook of a message? What a giant waste of time. If he knew where his mother was buried, why not go straight to the cops; get them to dig her up?'

Adam shrugged. 'I don't know. But he must have had a good reason.'

I said, 'I doubt whether a young black guy back then would have had much credibility with the cops in this part of the world anyway.'

We drove for a while, heading north, before Mack said, 'Anyway, for all we know, it's Sam in that grave there.'

Adam said, 'Sam's the guy I saw that day at the gate, with Bill. I'm sure of it now. Sam's the initiator of that coded message.'

Mack voiced what we were all thinking. 'Then let's go find the guy.'

We drove into Dallas with the optimistic belief we could find that house in the suburbs, but the optimism quickly dwindled as we drove back and forth for an hour through a maze of little streets. Adam kept saying, 'The courthouse…great gothic, red-brick building…', so we finally found the courthouse, but after that it became guesswork.

'Was it north, south, east or west of the courthouse, Adam?' I asked him.

'I wish I could be sure. Somewhere where you knew you were suddenly in a residential area.'

'There's thousands of residential areas in the suburbs of Dallas,' said Mack.

'A wall…tree or bush climbing up it…a little gate in the middle of it…quite a tall house…that's where I saw Sam....'

'Are you sure this wasn't one of your night-visions, Mr. R?' asked Mack.

We finally gave up. 'It's not serious,' said Adam. 'We've got almost the entire picture; we should be rejoicing.'

'It'd be great to have a witness though,' said Mack, 'a real, live, breathing witness, not one that's been mouldering in the earth for decades. Or do you aim to prop the skeleton on the witness stand, see what it has to say?' We laughed and went to get a hamburger.

'Anyway,' Adam finally said, as we headed back to our little town-house in Sherman, 'we could probably trace him at SMU or NTSU. Maybe even put an ad in the paper. He's bound to read about all this stuff if it comes to a trial.'

And that was that. We pulled in at the post-office in Sherman. Just enough time to send a telegram. Manhattan address.

*****

Adam and I lay together in bed at our place in Sherman that night, that lull before the storm, before the call to action awaiting us on the following day, when we were due to phone 'Wolf'. Adam said suddenly, 'D'you know why Charlene hates me so much?'

I knew it wasn't so much a question as the prelude to an explanation. I myself had always taken Charlene's attitude towards Adam for granted and assumed she hated him because she herself sided with Hateley. I said, 'It's because she's so close to Hateley, and Hateley clearly hates you.'

'No,' said Adam, 'that's why she's out to get me. You're right: what Hateley wants, she wants; their destinies seem for some reason inextricably mixed.' He paused. 'But that's not why she hates me.'

'Why then?'

A long pause followed before Adam replied quietly, 'Charlene once tried to seduce me. I'm in her bloodstream.' The statement took my breath away. It was made so casually, while the implications of it seemed so enormous. Adam continued, 'I rejected her. She can't forgive me for that. Charlene is not someone who takes rejection easily.' We lay for a moment or two in silence, before he added, 'You know, you're the first person I've ever told this to.'

'When was it, Adam?'

'Years ago. 1963, when I first went to Hillcrest.' He hesitated, as if it were something he'd rather forget, and then said quietly, 'In my small room at the school. Charlene happened to be in there for some reason - I think she'd come in from Williamson's room and then Williamson had vanished. I'd turned round to put another record on the record-player, and when I turned back she was on my bed taking her stockings off. Provocatively.'

'Did she fancy you, Adam?' The question jerked from me spontaneously.

'Maybe. I don't know. She never said; just continued to remove enough of her garb to make me suppose so. And I spurned her. The matter was never raised again after the incident. We just behaved as if it had never happened.' He paused and then added, 'Apparently the official pretext though was to find out if I was a homosexual. The question seemed of vital significance to the school's welfare.'

I couldn't help laughing. 'I suppose she thinks you are then, if you rejected her.'

'Perhaps. I don't know.'

Adam went silent again for a while. He was so quiet I thought he'd forgotten the matter. Then he said, 'We were lying on that little pull-out bed in my apartment; she'd removed quite a bit; we'd even got as far, I remember, as a clinch, when suddenly I'm reversing out of it: *'Charlene, I don't think this is going to work'. 'What's the matter? Don't you like sex?'* You can't imagine the scorn in her voice. She was still actually breathing hard, but I don't think it was from passion.'

I interrupted Adam involuntarily. 'Of course it wasn't...'

But Adam didn't let me finish. 'No, you're right, it wasn't. She was vulnerable, humiliated, that's the reason, struggling to regain control. '*Yes, Charlene, I like sex...*(I remember I was climbing off the bed, trying to find a strategy, make light of what had occurred)...*I like you too, but not in that way'*.' Adam lay now next to me, calmly reconstructing the events. 'She was on the edge of the bed re-assembling herself. I went over, took the Schubert off the record-player; a Schubert string quartet: "*Death and the Maiden*".' He laughed. 'There's an irony.'

I ignored his humour. 'Did she say anything else?'

'Yes, I suppose the gist of the matter.' He paused, clearly trying to remember precisely. 'I'd turned back from the record player, facing her and she whispered, '*You think you're so clever, don't you, Adam Riley, with your verbal gymnastics? Weasel words is what I call them.'* Then she edged past the desk until we were a yard or so apart, eyeing each other. *'I was only testing you out, you realise, Mr. Riley. And I think I've discovered all I needed to know.'* I didn't spend time trying to decipher any double meaning in her words. '*Look, Charlene, this little drama goes no further than these four walls; you can trust me. It's buried here as if it never happened. I think we've managed to pull the fat from the fire.'* I even attempted a reassuring smile, and whether it was this smile or some timbre in my voice, I can't be sure; she turned back from the door with an expression contorted with rage. She almost hissed the words, *'You little gay! If it was in my power, you'd be out on your neck tomorrow. You're a corrupting influence in this place.'* And she disappeared into the night.'

That was the end of his account, and as we lay for a second or two in the darkness, saying nothing, Adam uttered a kind of guttural laugh, an expulsion of breath, relief, as if yet one more burden had been lifted from his shoulders. I loved him for it. He made light of everything.

He'd rejected Charlene's advances and he found it amusing. He found everything amusing and then moved on. That was the way he was. And I genuinely believe he'd even felt sorry for Charlene at that moment, forgave her, tried to shoulder her shame. However, I was under no illusions that she felt the same about him; she was incapable of that. And she was dangerous. Adam's anecdote had given me even more reason to be cautious; her venom was personal, vengeful.

Adam fell quickly asleep and as I lay there in the darkness I knew I had to be watchful for him, to temper his seemingly irresistible desire to court danger, as if he considered himself invulnerable. I'd always loved him, but now things had changed with me and he'd become part of me. He was in *my* bloodstream.

Wolf

We were at the call-box next morning, all of us, half in and half out - Mack and I squeezed in as best we could, Adam, hand poised over the receiver, right inside the cabin. Adam had claimed this one for his own. Even though Mack had grumbled a bit, declaring he had 'first-hand knowledge of the likely course of the anticipated conversation' and that 'he'd earned, the right, by blood, toil and sweat, to be the first to break the good news to Wolfie', Adam had insisted on answering the call himself. His argument was a good one: 'So far as we know, Mack, Hateley isn't even aware of your presence - or Tessa's - in this whole business. Why implicate yourself unnecessarily then?'

The argument had held sway. So it was Adam, inside the kiosk, picking up the receiver as the call came in, precisely at 11.00 am. Adam, after a moment and speaking calmly into the mouth-piece, said, 'Hello, is that the Wolf?' We watched him wait expectantly, and then, one second later, examine the receiver in his hand, as if he expected Wolf to appear bodily down it. He uttered a muffled oath and replaced the receiver. 'He hung up!'

Dismay. No, not dismay, more than dismay: despair. This was our moment, and we'd blown it. Hateley had slipped out of our grasp; the trail had gone dead.

'He hung up,' repeated Adam.

'Perhaps that's all there is,' suggested Mack. 'Perhaps that's the way the Wolf and the Mongrel communicate.'

'In that case, why would they bother to speak on the phone?' I said. 'Why not just put it all in the telegram?'

'You're right,' said Adam, 'there must be a purpose for the phone-call; otherwise why all these passwords, names etc. So what did we do wrong?' We looked desperately at each other, seeking from somewhere a spark of inspiration.

'Perhaps that's it,' I said, looking at Adam. 'Perhaps it's the key we got wrong. The precise order of things. What *exactly* did he say on the phone just now?'

'Nothing. He just put the phone down. Nothing else.'

'Well maybe he speaks first in that case; when he says 'Wolf' you say the word 'Mongrel' back at him.'

'Maybe, maybe,' said Mack. 'There's lots of maybes as usual. Maybe that little shit on the mountain top omitted to tell us the vital password. And maybe that guy Hateley is right this minute tracing the call, so he can arrive here with a reception committee.'

Adam shrugged. 'Yes, maybe, but we haven't got anything else.'

'And maybe he won't call again either,' said Mack.

'Maybe.'

Tensely, we waited. Half an hour passed. Nothing.

'Shall we keep waiting?' said Adam.

I looked at my watch. 'Give it another half hour. We've got nothing to lose.'

'Except a violent death in a hail of machine-gun bullets.'

'Don't get over-dramatic, Mack. Hateley doesn't operate like that.' We waited silently. I checked my watch again. It was nearly mid-day, 12:00.

And then the phone rang again. Adam leapt into the booth and I shouted at the same time, 'Remember, Adam, just say Mongrel in response, and then wait.'

I reconstruct below, as closely as I can, the dialogue that took place between Adam and Hateley, based on Adam's own subsequent account and from what I was able to hear myself outside the phone-box.

- Wolf.
- Mongrel.
- Who is this?
- It's a voice from beyond the grave, Wolf.
- What's that meant to mean?
- It means the person you're speaking to is dead. (Pause). By rights. Except it didn't happen that way….
- Where's Mr. Denver?
- Are you referring to the little rat you sent to kill me? (Pause. No response). He met with an unfortunate accident. He's at dinner?
- How's that? What d'you mean 'at dinner'?
- Not where he eats, but where he's eaten.
- What the hell does that mean?
- Not only are you unfamiliar with your Shakespeare, Charlie, you also seem unfamiliar with your English grammar. (No response)….The phrase is a simple grammatical juggling with the active and passive voice. (No response)….May I recommend *Harbrace College Handbook*; it's an authoritative grammar of the English language.
- (Long pause). 'Are you alone?'
- That would be telling.
- Where are you right now?
- That would be telling.
- (Long pause. Adam feared he'd hung up, but he hadn't). What d'you want?
- Just reporting in, that's all. To let you know your secret's out….You're rumbled, Hateley.
- (Long pause). What secret's that?
- The secret you share with some of your associates. The one that has to do with Mr. Bill Jackson Jnr, a colleague and friend of mine.

- I thought as much; you're that little wise-guy teacher from the Hillcrest School.
- Correct. It took you long enough. And before you hang up I think you and I need to have a chat about Bill Jackson.
- What's there to chat about? I thought we'd heard the last of that little commie bastard.
- We have. But I think you know that yourself....Before Mr. 'Denver' met with his accident, he told me one or two things about the kind of work he does. And Mr. Jackson Jnr's name kept cropping up....Come to think of it, Mr. Jackson Snr's name was mentioned too, in the same connection.
- (Long pause, during which Hateley seemed to be conferring). You've got no proof of anything, Riley. And I don't suppose Denver's going to do much more talking anymore.
- Oh, but we *do* have proof. Letters, witnesses, messages.
- (More conferring). Nothing that isn't circumstantial.
- I'm not talking technicalities here, Hateley. I'm talking black and white. Firm evidence. Did you or did you not kill Bill Jackson Jnr of Austin, Texas.
- If I told you no, you wouldn't believe me; if I told you yes, no one else would believe me. I don't kill people, Riley. (pause). I don't think you've got a case to propose, nor I a case to answer.
- Let me rephrase: Did you commission the death of Bill Jackson Jnr?
- Same answer. Same dead end, I'm afraid.
- (Adam felt sure he would hang up). Don't hang up....There's one more thing: Does the name Sam Toms mean anything to you?
- (Hesitation. Conferring). Isn't he that little nigger boy servant used to work for Bill and Margaret Jackson. What about him? Seems to have gone off somewhere. Disappeared off the face of the earth.
- Why do you think that was?
- Hell knows. You'd better ask him yourself. But you ain't going to find him; there ain't nobody going to find that son-of-a-bitch.

- (Pause). I found his mother though.
- (Long pause). And where might that have been?
- Somewhere up in the Lake Texoma area. (Silence, so Adam continued)....She wasn't doing much...just lying around.
- (Hesitation). I think maybe we should meet, Riley.
- You can tell your little side-kick attorney, Philips, I've got no intention of meeting you anywhere, you murderous son-of-a-bitch!
- (Pause) What is it you want, Riley? Is it money?
- No, not money; justice, I suppose.
- Justice for a nigger woman?
- That's right....And just in case you get any ideas, either you or your associates, there are at least three signed unopened accounts of this whole business on the editorial desks of newspapers in three separate states, each with instructions they should be opened in the event of anything happening to me, personally.
- (Conferring). You're bluffing, Riley.
- Try me then.
- Nothing'll stand up in court.
- Sadie Toms certainly won't.
- No one will; that's your problem. (Pause). A jury might even be persuaded to believe this nigger fellow made it all up, maybe did his mother in himself.
- You're right, Wolf. Especially if it's white....But *I'm* coming after you. Each time you look around, I'll be there.

Uttering a string of obscenities and invective, Hateley finally hung up. It's been said we did the wrong thing alerting him, and in hindsight and given the tragic events that ensued, perhaps we did. But what alternative did we have? If we'd done nothing and waited for Hateley to come in search of us, it's likely the outcome would have been the same.

Adam emerged from the call-box tense and alert, but essentially very depressed. It was obvious to all of us that Hateley had a point, that we had nothing but the word of a young black student (who'd vanished) that any of this was true. Even if the police were to be persuaded to dig up Sadie Toms' remains, there'd be no evidence to pin the crime on Hateley and his crew. Without the presence of Sam, there could be no explanations, no motives, nothing.

Nevertheless, we sent off our completed testimony in sealed envelopes to Joe Verard and to three respected state newspapers: *the Kansas City Star*, *the Oklahoman*, *the Boston Globe*, and we waited, for no good reason other than that we didn't know what else to do. Perhaps, like a '*deus ex machina*', Sam Toms would appear from his hiding-place and, with a wave of his wand and a few plausible explanations, convert tragedy into comedy.

But nothing of course happened and we'd more or less decided, all three of us, to give up and go home - let Fate grind out its own implacable conclusion - when the unexpected arrival of James Williamson towards the end of that week ushered in a quite horrific chain of events. Now, even after a few months have passed, I can scarcely bring myself to think of that ultimate day at Hillcrest, let alone to account for it in writing - a dramatic denouement to our activities, as grotesque, solemn, and unreal as any to be found on the world's tragic stages.

Osric

It seems certain that in the three- or four-day interim, following the phone-call and before the arrival of Williamson, some kind of communication took place between Hateley and Charlene Mays, either by phone, mail or even in person. How else would Williamson have been commissioned to appear so abruptly with his summons?

We bumped into him in a Safeway supermarket in the centre of Sherman in the middle of the first week of September. By chance or by design on his part? Almost certainly the latter. Unseen, we watched him approach down the aisle, picking waspishly at items on the shelves and putting them in his basket, adjusting his glasses before strutting on.

'My god,' Adam said under his breath, 'the Water-fly approacheth.'

'It's Mr. Williamson,' I said with surprise, almost excitement, while Mack, suppressing outright laughter, managed a sort of cough. 'Yes, and one of your former colleagues, Mr. Riley.' He pretended to be shocked at Adam's frivolous mockery.

'That's for sure,' replied Adam earnestly, 'and you can bet he'll have something seriously unserious to say.'

'I thought you faculty all stuck together,' said Mack. 'Just shows how naïve I was.'

'We try, Mack; you're right. But this particular faculty member unfortunately always lacked a certain *gravitas*. Watch.'

By this time Mr. Williamson was upon us and took our suppressed laughter as a sign of greeting. 'Fancy bumping into you three in Safeway!' He scrutinised us solemnly, each in turn. 'Tessa Bellman, Mack Neumann, and Hamlet himself. As knavish a foreign trio of plotters as ever I saw.'

'What's 'foreign' about it, Mr. Williamson?' asked Mack.

Williamson feigned astonishment. 'Two Germans and a Dane. I thought we all once concurred - at that restaurant in Fort Worth I think it was - that Neumann and Bellman must be German of origin. And as for Hamlet, I rest my case. What brings the Prince of Denmark to these parts?'

'Alas, no longer the Hamlet you once knew, I'm afraid, James,' said Adam. 'Times have changed.'

'Oh dear. Have you come down in the world? On one of the last occasions we met, I distinctly remember you claiming ownership of Hamlet's spirit, if not his soul. Did his *persona* desert you?'

'No, I was probably just drunk.'

'You were. Intoxicated, and reincarnated as the great Prince himself.' He was shaken with a momentary spasm of laughter. 'You had also, as I remember, recently been involved in a demeaning wrestling match with one of the students.' Something at that moment - and for no apparent reason - sent a shudder through me, a deep sense of misgiving. These exaggerated references to Hamlet, Adam, a 'wrestling match', reminded me of something, but I couldn't put my finger on what.

'Jerry Coburt. Yes, you're right, Billy. I must have been intoxicated with the sense of victory.' Adam laughed and then made a big show of sighing deeply. 'But sadly those halcyon days are gone. We are summoned to more solemn matters.'

'Oh dear,' said Williamson. 'Have the harsh realities of life finally come home to roost?' He didn't wait for an answer. 'But then I never really thought Hamlet suited you. Too introspective, too self-obsessed. I, of course, preferred the less demanding role of Osric. And, of course, a whole lot more...shall we say... 'undramatic' an ending for him too; I'm sure you'll agree.' He shoved his glasses back onto his nose. 'But then, pride is often the prelude to a fall.'

'What *was* Osric's ending, Mr. Williamson?' asked Mack.

'Nobody knows. He was just conveniently forgotten by his author. Like most of us in real life, you could say.' He convulsed with delight at this brilliant show of wit.

In the silence that followed, and as Mr. Williamson picked a few more food items off the shelf, I hurriedly whispered to Adam, 'What fight was that? Was that the fight you had once with Jerry Coburt on the Breezeway?'

'On the grassy bank just below the Breezeway, yes,' replied Adam, also under his breath. 'There was nothing in it. The boys engineered it, after a soccer practice. It was good-humoured. Mack will remember.'

'I do,' said Mack. 'Mr. R took Jerry apart. Destroyed him. We were all impressed.'

'What was it for, Mack?' I asked hurriedly (Williamson was by now returning from his sortie down the aisle).

'Nothing. It was a 'bout', that's all. A bit of fun.'

Williamson joined us, and I said, 'How's Hillcrest, Mr. Williamson? Are you doing the shopping for Charlene? Term's not started yet, has it? I wonder she's not here with you.'

'Good heavens no. Mrs. Mays is much too high and mighty to do anything as menial as shopping these days.' The mention of Charlene seemed to have jogged his memory. 'But that reminds me, I almost forgot. Talking of shopping...*and* talking of wrestling for that matter... *and* talking of Charlene (now, back to his old, witty self, he writhed like a whipped cobra), I have a commission from Charlene. And to you, no less.' He glanced deliberately at Adam. 'There's to be an 'open' day at Hillcrest this weekend to kick the academic year off with a bang, so to speak, a 'Games-day' they're calling it, a new highlight in the competitive calendar, and *you* (he turned back to Adam) are invited. Charlene asked me to make sure you'd be there.'

In the lengthy pause that followed, Mack asked, 'And what about *us*?'

Williamson replied, 'I don't think she's expecting *you*.'

'Well we're coming anyway.' The vehemence of the remark took Williamson by surprise. He had no answer.

Adam said, 'What does this 'Games-day' consist of, Billy?'

'Let me see, (he paused for effect)…a soccer game - faculty, past and present, versus the alumni.' He brushed a piece of fluff from his sleeve, and for a moment preened himself like a peacock. 'A soccer match, let me say, in which *I* personally will most certainly not be taking part.'

Adam said, 'You were never exactly one for rough sporting participation were you, Billy?'

'I certainly wasn't. Nor am I now. Let me see…where was I? Oh yes, the soccer game is to be followed by a wrestling contest in….'

Mack interrupted him in mid-flow. '…A wrestling contest, for heaven's sake!'

Mentally winded for a second, Williamson struggled for composure. 'Yes,' he finally proclaimed (a medieval herald addressing his awe-struck audience) 'a wrestling contest…a wrestling contest in which…in which….'

He'd apparently forgotten the rest. Adam prompted him. 'Between whom, Billy, this contest?'

'Oh yes, all faculty, new or old, under the age of 25, are challenged to wrestle with a selected school 'champion'…a veritable trial by ordeal…a contest the like of which…the like of which….'

Adam muttered, 'He's forgotten his lines again.'

'…the like of which hasn't occurred since David fought with Goliath….' Williamson collapsed in a spasm of laughter, overcome by his performance.

'Which one is David and which Goliath?' asked Mack.

Williamson looked confused and had no answer. Mack said, 'If it's under 25, it could include you too, Mr. Williamson. Are you intending to wrestle?'

'No,' he insisted, 'I am to judge the contest.'

'Whose idea is this ridiculous rigmarole, Billy?' asked Adam.

'Charlene's, of course. She makes all the decisions these days. There's to be a *victor ludorum*, chosen by Charlene, followed by a barbecue.' He looked at his watch. 'I must be going.' Then he said, looking intently at Adam, 'But between you, me and the gatepost, Mr. Slater and Mrs. Mays probably just want to offer you your job back.'

We watched the 'water-fly' strut off down the aisle, backside swaying.

Once he was out of hearing, Mack said earnestly, 'Don't go, Mr. R. It's a trick; that devious witch has got something up her sleeve.' And I added, 'Adam, it's obvious, Charlene must have heard about that fight with Jerry Coburt back then. It's bound to have reached her ears. She's planning something. She's using you. Please don't get involved in this 'contest'.'

'You may be right, but I confess I look forward to the chance of wrestling with Jerry Coburt again. I'll still beat him.'

His bravado was lost on Mack and me; it was already clear to both of us he was walking into a carefully-laid trap. 'Don't go, Adam.' I echoed Mack's plea.

'What else can we do?' replied Adam. 'We've reached an impasse here. This is perhaps our one chance of confronting the lot of them in one fell swoop. Hateley's bound to be there, Faulkner, all of them.' Adam noticed our hesitation and continued, 'Look, We don't really have a choice. We've gone this far; we have to carry it through. And realistically, what's Hateley going to try to pull with all those people there? A mass suicide pact on the field of play?' While we stood there uncertainly, he added flippantly, 'In the traditions of true 'cultish' procedure?'

He was right. The logic seemed indisputable; Williamson's mission already appeared to be resembling a fairy-tale. It was reluctantly decided we'd go. Mack said, 'If you're going, Mr. R, then *I'm* certainly going. But discreetly. I'll take part in the soccer and then I'll fade into the background. No one'll even know I'm there.'

I said straightaway, 'Then where do you plan to be, Mack?'

'Have you ever watched those bodyguards in movies or news-clips? They blend into the crowd; that is until something goes wrong. In the crowd, that's where I plan to be.'

'Right, Mack, you do that,' said Adam; 'makes me feel important to have my own real, live bodyguard. I suppose this is another accomplishment you learned from your uncle in Wyoming.'

'Hasn't let you down yet, Mr. R. But don't joke; this is *real* danger, just as real as up there on the mountain. We've got this far; I'm not going to let any new homicidal maniac put a bullet in you. I'm going to wire you up.'

'You're going to do *what*?' said Adam.

Mack looked hard at him. 'Surveillance. We'll hide a mic on you; I'm going to listen into every spook who comes near.'

'What sort of a mic?'

'It's like a mini walkie-talkie. Don't worry; trust me.'

Adam smiled uncertainly. 'Have it your own way, Mack. I do trust you.' Then he said something unexpected, something that startled me, 'But to be honest, I'm tired of this endless pursuit. It's taken over my life; I'm no longer the same person. Now is the time for it to end. One way or another. I almost don't care which.'

Mack responded earnestly, 'We'll look after you, Mr. R. We're not going to let anything happen to you.'

It was decided, and, back in Sherman, we waited with growing impatience for the weekend.

Denouement

Sunday, September 3rd 1967 was a splendid day, warm, but with a slight breeze, and the School basked in the predictable early September sunshine. Hillcrest Registration Day that year, I remember, was, as a marketing exercise, bold and aggressive in its conception. There were signs at Reception welcoming new students (and parents) to Registration, pointing the way to the new girls' dorm down the hill (at last completed, during the summer vacation apparently), and down to the various athletic events out on the field. The whole campus looked clean and tidy. Hillcrest had put on its smartest shirt front.

However, on first impression, the 'Games-day' itself didn't seem to be the grandiose spectacle predicted by Mr. Williamson (but then, do people ever imagine events realistically, guided as they are by their own secret needs and desires?). No, at first sight anyway, the whole day was conceived on a far more modest scale than Williamson's dreams, less competitive, less dramatic, entirely in keeping with the old Hillcrest spirit of participation for all, and in which there are neither winners nor losers. It was simply a fun-day, or so it appeared. There were races for the kiddies and events to suit all ages. Sure, there *was* a soccer match, an unskilful, somewhat ill-tempered affair on the new soccer pitch, and sure there was to be wrestling for those that fancied it, but there was a whole lot more: in the south-west corner, parents and students were invited to go practise their homespun skills at the baseball cage and mound; on the basket-ball court, on the far side of the school, for the price of a dollar, fathers and sons could chuck baskets and win prizes; there was even croquet on offer, on a new, well-watered lawn at the back of Jim Slater's apartment. An entire sports-circuit, in other words, for all to enjoy.

But beneath this facade of the old Hillcrest - this non-competitive, modest mask - subtle changes, subtle markers were evident to those of us who'd known it as it was: the steady procession of Cadillacs gliding up to Reception throughout the morning, occupants tumbling out to take a peek at this go-ahead school in it unique and beautiful setting, its novel open-day, some parents even ready, on-the-spot, to enrol their cowed sons and daughters for the up-coming Fall term. There was brashness about the place we'd never known in '63. New facilities had begun to spring up on what once had been open fields: evidence of a vast new sports complex arising from the prairie, a brand new art-school, domed like an observatory and now standing proudly in what had once been an obscure little corner beyond the basket-ball court; there were signs to the new girls' dorm down the hill, building plans and designs for other parts of the campus on display at Reception, which revealed ambitious schemes for a new library, an assembly hall on the site of the old basket-ball court, a new dining-hall, a large swimming-pool. Money was talking. It smacked of glitz and glamour, a far cry from that honest, participatory endeavour called 'Education' I remembered and loved about Hillcrest.

'Plunging ever deeper, ever more recklessly, into hock to its dubious financiers,' whispered Adam, as we took in the scene at the top of the slope down to the playing-fields, where once had been the simple entrance to the Breezeway but was now the site of a lavish new Reception area.

And here now approaching us, came the high priestess, the orchestrator of all these changes: Charlene, resplendent in a flowery dress to match the brilliant colour of the occasion. Adam whispered to me, 'I wonder what happened to our humble cook in her long black skirt, stained with the fat of countless dinners.' But he smiled as she approached, and said, 'I love your new plans, Charlene. For the school, I mean.'

Charlene threw him a quizzical glance, as if doubting his sincerity, then said in that strangely thin, lilting voice of hers, 'Things have changed since you were here, Adam Riley. We have to move with the times, don't we?'

'What times would they be, Charlene?'

'There's lots of money in Texas at the moment. The economy is booming. It would be a shame not to cash in on it, wouldn't it? By the way, that reminds me, you need to talk to Jim. He's got some proposals to share with you.'

Her behaviour and words struck me as ambiguous. Wasn't it she herself, according to Mr. Williamson, who was hoping to see Adam at this event? Why now so casually, almost off-handedly, pointing the way towards Jim Slater? Was this some double-game they were playing? I suspected so.

At Charlene's proposal, Adam assumed an air of surprise. 'I wonder what he can want. Thanks, Charlene, I'll have a word with him later.'

'This afternoon would be a good moment; we're having a barbecue out on the new patio.'

'Forgive my ignorance, Charlene. Where is that?'

Charlene gave him a look of mock surprise. 'At the back of the Headmaster's new apartment of course. Where else?'

Adam feigned surprise too. 'My, how things have moved on in my absence.'

She looked at him, wide-eyed. 'Yes, there is life beyond Adam Riley after all.' The silent animosity between them was intense. I could see and understand now how the matter went beyond pure professional differences.

Charlene glanced in my direction, pretending to notice my presence for the first time. 'Tessa darling, how nice to see you. And what are you up to these days? Haven't you been in London this past year?'

I was preparing to answer, but she'd already swept off towards the games-field. Adam and I watched her for a while in silence, surrounded as she immediately was by a crowd of admiring parents and friends. 'Two-timing bastard,' said Adam.

I looked at him earnestly. 'Adam, whatever you do today, don't trust Charlene. I've got an uneasy feeling about her. She doesn't intend any good towards you.'

'I *don't* trust her; I never did. What's changed?'

'*She's* changed somehow, Adam.' He seemed momentarily to hesitate, so I added, 'It's a woman thing. I feel it in my guts. Please believe me.'

'No, she's always been like that. It's just you didn't know it. We faculty did. And now she no longer has to hide her spleen. The school has changed with her. Her star's in the ascendancy.'

In view of what happened later that day, I remember that moment as the final chance to rein in Adam's ingenuous self-confidence. But Charlene must have known him better; she knew there was no reining him in. *Adam Riley never could resist a challenge*. She knew that; Adam himself didn't.

We were watching Charlene in the distance, pinning a rosette on a little kid's shirt. Beside her stood quite a tall, imposing figure, whom none of us at first recognised until suddenly the words: *My god!* jerked from my mouth involuntarily.

'What's the matter, Tessa?' said Mack.

'It's George. My brother! With Charlene.'

There was a moment's hesitation before Adam said, 'Well, you'd better go and speak to him.'

I remember recoiling at the thought, the possibilities of antagonism and outright violence George had hinted at in his letters still fresh in my mind, but it was too late anyway, out of our hands, for George, following an indication by Charlene, was already walking in our direction.

'George,' I said as he approached, 'what are you doing here?'

'Not pleased to see me, sis?' he said. 'It figures.'

'Of course I'm pleased to see you. But I never expected it would be at Hillcrest.'

'Why not? Am I not the school's official doctor? I get invited to such events.'

As I looked at him, amazed, he added, 'I'm an intern at the Denber main hospital. Didn't you know? A registrar. Hence my connection with Hillcrest.'

'No, I didn't know, George,' I said. 'How could I? You never tell us anything.'

George, retreating now into that remote and secret corner none of us could ever reach, said, 'As you know, I find people a distraction.'

'Distraction from what?' Mack couldn't resist asking.

George gave him a blank stare. 'Ones own momentum of course, ones career.'

'I thought people were important for ones career,' countered Mack.

George's withering stare went slowly from Mack to me, and then Adam, who was standing a couple of paces behind me. 'Yes, the *right* people, I suppose.'

'Isn't your own sister one of the 'right' people?'

'Unfortunately not. My sister's headstrong, to her own detriment, and happens to surround herself with the *wrong* people.'

'Of which I suppose I'm one,' said Mack, growing impatient.

George eyed Mack with all that condescension I knew so well (how little my brother appeared to have changed). 'If - as I assume - you're one of my worthless sister's entourage, then yes, I find you an irrelevance.'

They stood there for a second or two, glaring at each other, two adversaries on the edge of physical confrontation.

I intervened. 'Who *is* relevant to you, George? Anyone?'

'Yes, sis, it's simple.' He reflected for a moment. 'As I've often told you (and the family): people in my speciality who can further my career are relevant to me. Colleagues ....'

For a moment, I found myself remembering a hot summer's evening a few years ago, all of us sitting around reading Shakespeare, a younger George seething all evening with callous indifference. 'You haven't changed a bit, have you, George?'

'No, sis, and I hope I don't.' We were looking at each other again across a gulf of irreconcilability.

'And what *is* this precious specialty you're so keen to further?' asked Mack, breaking the spell.

George glanced quickly at him. 'Not that it need concern you, whoever you happen to be, nor anyone else for that matter...' he looked directly at each of us in turn '...but I specialise in breathing. Lungs, lung infections, pneumonia, that sort of thing.' He smiled faintly, and continued, 'My goal, you see, is to be a consultant in that quite important - in certain cases rather unfortunate - need people seem to have, to draw breath.'

This final slight was clearly aimed at Mack, who turned away and said to Adam and me, 'I'm off, you two, to do my bit in the soccer and after that you'll find me up in the boys' dorm. I have things to see to, to set up.' And with that, he left.

It was at this point that George pretended to notice Adam, who'd been standing all this while in the background saying little, perhaps hoping to avoid a confrontation. 'I know precisely who you are,' my brother said, 'even though we've scarcely met. You're that head-in-the-clouds dabbler in paltry theatrical productions, aren't you?'

It was more a statement than a question, and Adam simply nodded and replied almost under his breath, 'Maybe.'

'Child molester too, perhaps?' George added, raising his eyebrows a fraction and indicating me.

Such provocation was impossible to bear, and Adam said quietly, 'George, your sister is not a child.'

'More's the pity. I was hoping I'd be able to get the law on you.' And then he added enigmatically, 'But so be it. I suppose one must find other means of fitting the punishment to the crime.'

'What crime is that, George?' I said, starting to feel all my old hostility towards this patronising brother.

'Your pregnancy of course. What else? Your dishonouring of our family name and your ruining of your own life and future. Nothing more serious than that though.'

The same old sarcasm and disrespect. It was all out in the open now. But Adam, in spite of my brother's outright hostility towards him, still continued to say little, refused to be drawn in.

'George, my life is my own,' I said firmly. You're not my keeper. You don't need to be my keeper. I'm my own keeper. I can decide my own future.'

'It seems obvious you can't, Tessa. It's people like this dreamer here who get in the way.' He looked hard at me, a cold stare running up and down the length of my body. 'What are you planning to do? A single mother. With a child to take care of. All chances of a career thrown out of the window. No prospects, no honour. Yes, you do need a keeper.'

As he talked, I was growing more and more angry. 'George,' I shouted at last, 'who might that keeper be? Yourself, with your calculating schemes towards self-betterment? I don't need your diagnoses, nor your help. You never grew up. You were right when you said that once, and it's clear now that you *haven't* grown up.' I paused, wondering what to say next, and then suddenly knew for certain. 'Leave Adam out of this. This is *my* child. My responsibility. It's me bringing this child into the world, no one else. And I will love it.' Again I hesitated and then continued, 'How much more maturity do you want? How much more grown up must one be to fit your marvellous scheme of things?'

George clearly hadn't expected my outburst, had supposed he had the field to himself. He appeared stunned, ready to retreat back into his old shell. For a moment, I thought he was going to walk off, but instead he said simply, 'You can't have this child, Tessa. It will need to be aborted.'

'I love it,' I screamed. 'I love it now and I will love it when it comes.'

It was at this moment Adam decided to intervene. Never had I heard him speak so clearly, so calmly. It was as if all the divergent and discordant things within him were at last resolving themselves. 'George, don't worry; I will look after Tessa's child. *My* child. I love Tessa and we had a child together. We knew what we were doing then, and we know what we're doing now. And as for the family honour, everyone knows such thoughts are old-fashioned. But if it's what you desire, then I will marry Tess.' He paused before adding slowly and deliberately, 'For reasons honestly unknown to me, I have offended you. But it's time for reconciliation, to stop harbouring thoughts towards each other which have no substance, and to let the past be in the past.' He held out his hand. 'Please take my hand and let's make our peace and hope one day we will be not just friends but brothers.'

George, who had listened intently to this impassioned plea, remained expressionless. 'I would indeed like to believe you, Adam, but things will always be as they are, and unfortunately I will need firmer guarantees than mere words. You were clearly always very good with words.' Then, refusing to take Adam's offered hand, he said almost as if to himself, 'If I have indeed treated you unjustly, only time will tell.' And he strode away down the hill.

We watched him go and looked at each other uncertainly. Finally Adam said, 'He's hand in fist with Charlene. And what did he mean with that remark about '*finding other means of fitting the punishment to the crime*'?'

'Well we know what the crime is, but not the punishment. It's typical George; he's always been like that.'

We stood together, downcast, watching the excited mass of visitors enjoying the 'Games', and unsure what to do next.

'Tessa, c'mon,' said Adam at last. 'Don't let your brother ruin a rather amusing day. I don't give a damn about your brother really; nor Charlene for that matter. Let's go and do one of her '*sports circuits'*. Play them at their own game. Then that jumped-up little duchess will have to pin a rosette on me too.'

Adam had already forgotten what we'd all agreed earlier. *Be careful, be cautious*. And Mack had already left, quietly, for the boys' dorm, to set up his equipment. I wished he were with us then, to lend another persuasive voice. But Adam was already striding out towards the school basket-ball court. 'What on earth am I expected to do with this contraption (he was fingering the little microphone Mack had given him to keep in his breast pocket *at all times*)? How am I expected to fight a wrestling match with this in my pocket?'

'Don't fight the wrestling match then,' I said quickly. 'It's Charlene's idea. It's all stage-managed.'

'How can I back out of that now? Anyway, the Water-fly's going to come buzzing around. Roping me in. It's bound to be his big moment.'

'Adam,' I said, 'forget Water-fly, forget Charlene. Just keep a low profile. Find out from Mr. Slater what his so-called 'proposal' is and then let's go. This is the lion's den, don't you see?'

'I'll talk to Slater, but I doubt whether he knows what's pulling off anyway. I don't think he's in charge anymore.'

'Then let's just go now; we don't have to stay. Let's find Mack and disappear.'

But it wasn't to be like that. We all, that afternoon, seemed to have relinquished our will and our common-sense, and were swept along like jetsam on the tide of events. It was as if our return to Hillcrest had set in motion a whole chain of events over which we no longer had any control. The place, the personages, the circumstances, the timing: all were contriving to bring about an inevitable calamity.

I tried once more. 'Adam, I guarantee your bout will be the only one. It's not a 'tradition' or anything like that. It's all manipulated to get you centre stage, to make you feel good and then you'll drop your guard.' As I said it though, I knew he already had, that it was already too late. But I still urged him, 'Don't humour Charlene. Don't play into her hands. Let's just leave now.'

Adam wasn't listening. 'Tessa, could you just hold this microphone during the bout? Mack won't want to hear our groans and grunts anyway.' He was like someone sleep-walking.

How could one ever forget that wrestling match? That macabre spectacle of two young men locked in an absurd and unnecessary trial of strength, as if in some medieval lists?

Adam's bout predictably *was* the only bout; his impromptu and successful fight four years before with Jerry Coburt would not have escaped Charlene's notice, and a ridiculous public spectacle such as this suited her plans perfectly. We were gathered - faculty, students, curious parents - round a sort of ring, a small roped-off area at the top end of the field opposite the dining-hall, and no one was taking it seriously at first. People were talking excitedly, laughing, enjoying the prospect of a contest, and here was our MC, our judge, our referee, the Water-fly, skipping into the centre of the ring like a fairy. 'Let our champions appear!'

Adam stepped into the circle and then, macabre beyond all imagining, Charlene moved forward to the edge of the ring, leading by the arm a second wrestler, face concealed in the traditional hooded mask wrestlers sometimes wear to hide their identity, and she announced in that thin, piping voice of hers, 'I present my own champion on this day, and as surety of his success, I hereby wager a valuable necklace in expectation of his victory.' As gasps rang round the assembled circle of spectators, she removed from around her neck a gold necklace with a single ruby suspended from it, and handed it to Williamson. 'May the best man win, and, in token, reclaim his honour and this priceless jewel.'

I watched her 'champion' step into the circle and face Adam. There was something familiar about him - his build perhaps (clearly no boy), the manner in which he held himself, his walk - that reminded me of someone else, but the mask concealed the upper part of his face, and I assumed, for no good reason, this was Jerry Coburt, grown stronger and taller in the intervening years. Meanwhile, Adam stood warily watching his opponent, seemingly as surprised as all of us at this pageant-like course of events.

'Competitors will fight for a maximum of three minutes,' proclaimed Williamson. 'The winner will hold his opponent down for thirty seconds, shoulders touching the ground.'

At what precise point did that good-humoured, apparently harmless spectacle regress into a primitive rite? Even Adam and his opponent seemed to be enjoying it at first; on each of their lips, as they stood waiting, lay a sheepish grin, as if neither was really concerned about who won or who lost. But there's something essential about a contest that makes one take sides.

'When I throw my handkerchief into the ring, contestants touch hands and start fighting.'

There was a murmur of approval from the spectators, the Water-fly dodged back out of the way and his handkerchief fluttered into the ring. The wrestlers made their first tentative contact, almost casually, almost with embarrassment, as if neither could believe this was really happening. They stood, fingers locked together for several seconds, and made a few hasty grabs and thrusts that came to nothing.

I heard the first shout from somewhere at the back of the spectators: 'Come on Jerry!', and suddenly there were more shouts of encouragement, 'C'mon Jerry, c'mon Adam!' The two competitors stepped back, surprised, as if caught red-handed. Williamson screeched, 'Contestants, stay inside the ropes!', and the two of them came together again, this time with more deliberate intent. Already I could see, as they stood grasping each other, and with their lips set in increasing determination, that this was an uneven contest. Adam was simply stronger, more balanced, using only half his strength.

And all at once, in a frantic burst of sudden energy, they were both on the ground, arms and legs flailing, both furiously, recklessly, desperately fighting, and I realised Adam had got his headlock, one arm tight round Coburt's neck, and I was screaming in joy and excitement, 'C'mon Adam! C'mon Adam!' intent, in that moment, on my man winning at whatever the cost. It was unadorned bloodlust. Everyone was now shouting, and Adam still gripped his opponent in a vice, while Jerry kicked and lunged in an effort to free himself. The two of them, I realised, had entered a dimension we couldn't reach.

Something had to be done. I looked at Mr. Williamson, but he appeared paralysed, transfixed by the moment, unwilling to commit himself to a decision and to stop it. Desperately, I tried to shout above the din, but it was no use. At last I pushed my way through the ring of spectators and knelt by Adam, trying to unlock his grip, whispering, 'It's okay, you guys. The fight's over.' I heard some booing in the crowd. 'Adam, Adam,' I shouted above the noise, 'you've won. It's all right. It's finished.' Adam glanced up and our eyes met, but in his, no recognition. In that look, I glimpsed all the efforts, and uncertainties and fear and tension and disappointments of the past month spiralling down to this solitary moment where he sat on the grass, arm locked round his enemy's head. It was his victory. '*Adam, stop fighting*!' I screamed.

And at last he seemed to come back from a great distance away, and relaxed his grip, while Jerry struggled out from under him. The ineffective Williamson too had at last snapped out of paralysis, and was eager not to miss his own moment of glory. He ceremoniously threw a second handkerchief into the ring and strutted over to the two fighters. 'The bout is over. I proclaim the winner!'

Both contestants were now on their feet, shuffling like two sleep-walkers awakened prematurely. Williamson raised Adam's arm in the air. 'Adam Riley!'

There was a burst of applause, and then, still holding Adam's arm, and because he never could resist a jest, Williamson said something really absurd, 'Our latter-day Hamlet!' Laughter and some subdued cheers, although it was plain only very few of us could have understood the reference.

And now the queen of the festivities, in her flowery dress, was stepping forward to hang a medallion around Adam's neck. Holding the shiny metal in the air, she read out, '*Victor Ludorum, Hillcrest Games-day 1967*'. More clapping, and then, with one smooth movement, she peeled off the medieval mask of her 'champion' to reveal the smiling face beneath.

'That's not Jerry Coburt; that's my brother, George!' The words sprang to my lips, but no sound came out, while someone else called from the other side of the circle, 'Gee, Jerry, you sure have changed.' Charlene, revelling in the limelight and her clever deception, announced, 'Tea will be served out on the new patio.'

It's only after these intervening months that I've started to understand the subtle method that lay behind this madness, how we were all dancing to Charlene's tune that day, that even the critical substitution of Jerry Coburt for my brother in the wrestling contest had left me spellbound and speechless when I should have spoken out. We seemed under a spell. We were somnambulists, applauding wildly the conclusion of an event that should never have taken place. Had she said jump, that afternoon, we'd all have jumped.

And now the afternoon became early evening. The sun had started its slow descent into the prairie beyond Slater's new apartment. Tea was followed by drinks and a barbecue on his private patio, and then people started drifting away. Adam managed at last to collar Jim Slater, jubilant from the success of the day and already slightly tipsy. I too was on the patio with a few of my own friends - Sara, Susie, Monty, Jerry, Pride - who would later drift away too. Charlene came over and handed me a note at some point in the early evening, before whispering in my ear, 'I see you and Adam are obviously an item, so join us for dinner later, Darling.' The note, written in Mrs. Mays' neat hand, read: *'Victors' dinner. Please attend this informal celebration in the Headmaster's apartment at 8:00'.*

The invitation caused much amusement among my friends. I saw Charlene also hand a similar slip to Adam. But Adam was locked in conversation with his erstwhile boss, Jim Slater. We have a record of their conversation because Mack, who'd still not re-appeared and was still closeted somewhere in the boys' dorm, was recording everything through the microphone in Adam's breast-pocket.

- Adam, come back to Hillcrest. There's a job for you here; the school has more money, and we'd be in a position to offer you an improved salary, possibly improved accommodation.
- D'you mean, Jim, I could have this rather fine apartment right here?
- (Laughter) Uhh…Well, not quite *that* improved…. By the way, congratulations on your feats today on the field of combat. Most exciting. Uhh…as I was saying, Hillcrest has a vacancy for a French teacher and an assistant to Robert Akens in the boys' dorm.
- In other words, Jim, I can have my old job back.
- (Laughter). Well, that's about the sum of it, I suppose. But of course on a more permanent basis this time.
- Why would it be any more permanent this time, Jim?
- Uhh…well Hillcrest's thriving at the moment, registration is up, we've got an exciting new building program underway. I expect you've noticed…
- (Interrupting)...No, Jim, I don't think you understand. I'm not referring to the facilities, the external trappings shall we call them; they were fine the last time, exciting, innovative, unique. No, it was the spirit that drove me away in '65.

- What spirit are you referring to?
- The guiding spirit. The spirit which moves in a mysterious way; unfortunately not mysterious enough in this case, but all too plain and visible to those with an eye to see it.
- (Long hesitation)…I presume you're referring to the management of the school…uhh…the administration.
- The Board isn't a bad word for it, Jim. Yes, I'm referring to the running of the school. That's what drove me away last time. Under a cloud, if you remember, for too much supporting of Bill Jackson, who in turn was drummed out by this self-same Board for too much supporting of Joe Verard….
- (Blustering) Oh, Bill had what was coming to him….
- Did he have murder coming to him then? Did he deserve murder? (lengthy pause). Those self-same people who falsely accused Bill at that time, now have a far more serious charge to answer.
- (Blustering) What on earth do you mean? What possible evidence do you have for accusations of that kind? If you're referring to Bill's sad and untimely suicide, then…
- (Interruption). Jim, the evidence we have now suggests it wasn't suicide at all. It was murder….
- (Exploding) Preposterous! And who are you referring to by 'we' anyway?
- I'm not prepared to reveal that. Not yet. But Jim, you need to open your eyes. Your Board - the guiding spirit that moves upon these particular waters, the ones who were prepared to drum Bill out back then on a set of false charges - is rotten to the very core, and we have it - *I* have it - on good report, and on solid evidence, that some of the leading lights of that Board are certainly guilty, in law, of conspiracy to murder and indeed others of murder itself. (Very lengthy pause, punctuated by plenty of background noise from happy and inebriated guests). Jim, I'm off to get another beer…can I get you one? Don't go away; I haven't finished yet…(two minutes at least of background conversation, after which Adam takes up the conversation)…Jim, let's cut to the chase ….

- Uhh…I must warn you first that the allegations you've just made are both untrue and almost certainly libelous. Murdered by whom? Who precisely are you pointing the finger at?
- It'll come out in due course, but let me just say this: I could only, can only, come back to Hillcrest on the basis of your sacking the entire Board of governors and starting again with a clean sheet….

At this point the private conversation is unfortunately interrupted by the gentle voice of Charlene, summoning both Slater and Adam to the ceremony inside the apartment. We will never know how this conversation would have proceeded, but can only assume Adam and Slater agreed to differ and that, despite Adam's earlier accusations and ultimatum, they took their beers inside amicably enough, sat together at table and Slater, during the dinner, continued to solicit Adam to resume his old post on the faculty for the forthcoming term. Sixty minutes later, Slater lay dead. But such is Texas.

Charlene, determined as she was in her frantic pursuit of a supposedly more dynamic and forward-looking Hillcrest, had also, clearly unbeknown to her husband, decided to '*start again with a clean sheet*'. No longer the antiquated and outmoded educational practices of former years. There was to be no more room for the Jacksons, the Akens's, the Rileys (but then Adam Riley was, for her, already an altogether different proposition anyway). Her way was to be the future. Education could be bought, like any other product. And as if to emphasize this ruthless vision, Stanley Foreman had already been replaced as Chairman by Hateley, now seated at the head of the table next to Charlene (her position there guaranteed both as hostess for the dinner and '*First Lady of the Games*').

But none of these educational intentions, nor her secret plans and machinations, did we fully realise as we sat down to dinner. Sure we'd guessed she was up to something, but we'd been so lulled by the vibrancy of the entire event, the alcohol, the sunshine, that we never thought the execution of these 'intentions' would be here, and now, today. Sitting there at the top of the long, sumptuous table, flanked by Hateley on one side, my brother strangely on the other (Slater was down the other end, next to Adam), she announced we should serve ourselves from the side-table, buffet-style. Her usual amazing meal: three enormous salmon, cooked so the flesh was firm but succulent, with dressings, toppings, salads of various kinds; spicy chicken, cold red beef, kidney beans, rice for those who weren't partial to fish, or those with giant appetites, who could manage both menus. The food was literally spilling off the table. And wine within generous arm's length of every diner. We were all quickly intoxicated. And then it happened.

At the end of the first course, Charlene stood and carefully removed a fine linen cloth from an imposing chalice, a goblet, in front of her on the table.

'As first lady of these ceremonies,' she uttered in her clipped, soft-spoken voice, 'it's my pleasure and duty to announce our *Victor Ludorum* for the Games of '67.' Was she going to make a speech? We all strained to hear. 'In recognition of his outstanding skills on the soccer pitch, his enthralling wrestling bout, and (she paused for effect) not to mention his virtuosity on the croquet lawn (laughter)... the basket-ball court...the baseball cage...I'm delighted to present a former faculty member at Hillcrest and one who I hope will grace these Games for many years to come (we literally held our breath, although I already knew who it must be)...Adam Riley.'

Smiling, she looked down the long table at Adam, and carefully raised the imposing chalice, which stood before her. (In hindsight, what bold, almost reckless presumption! How could she have hoped to get away with it?). 'The Chairman of the Board (she indicated Hateley with a nod of the head), and our distinguished guest on my left here, our school medical officer...unfortunately our loser this year in the wrestling contest (polite laughter)... would like to join me in drinking to our *Victor Ludorum*.' She raised the chalice, drank and handed it in turn to Hateley and then to my brother. (What could my brother be doing, if not to hasten the downfall of Adam? He must have been in on it. He cannot be guiltless. Why else would he have been sitting at the top table, drinking from the cup? And as I write this, I hate him implacably for all that ensued that evening).

Charlene took the cup back and held it up. 'You see, Adam, your cup, already inscribed with your name on it.' On the chalice was a small silver plate with some writing on it. Charlene read, '*Adam Riley - Victor Ludorum 1967'*. (Applause and cheers). Charlene added, 'By courtesy of the local Wal-Mart.' (General laughter).

At this point, I remember, as if on cue, Williamson stepped forward and handed to her the delicate necklace with its precious ruby pendant (oh treachery!). 'My pledge to the winner of the wrestling contest,' she exclaimed. 'I throw it now into the cup.' She carefully dropped the necklace into the chalice.

Why was it that only now something stirred in my memory, something from somewhere else? I knew by heart this charade, from another context, but couldn't place it. I should have stepped forward, caused a pandemonium, stopped this grotesque ritual in its tracks, but I lamely sat and watched it happen, as if rooted to the spot.

Charlene now took the small cloth from beside her on the table, wiped the chalice, and sent it on its way down the table to Adam, via the line of seated and applauding guests. It was cunningly done; no one else in that room would have been presumptuous enough, under the circumstances, to drink from the cup as it passed from hand to hand, and Adam, awaiting its arrival, must have felt irresistibly impelled, by twenty sets of admiring eyes, to place it to his lips.

'I'd like you to drink, Adam, to Hillcrest and its future.' He did. As the cup touched his lips, and everybody joined in the clapping, me included, Adam seemed momentarily to hesitate before joining into the spirit of the occasion and drinking, even spilling some of the liquid in his haste.

How had it come to this? Drinking ceremoniously with ones avowed enemies? Of course, I don't doubt Adam's sincerity, just his overweening confidence: he *was* bent upon exposing them, I'm certain of that, but not right then and there; he was waiting for another time and place to bring his charges. But aren't we all victims of delay and hesitation?

What occurred next though, not even the wily Charlene could have predicted. Slater, next to Adam and already mildly drunk, pushed back his chair in an impetuous movement and got unsteadily to his feet. 'Uhh...I think, don't you, that as Headmaster of this establishment, I should at very least have the chance to be included in the official prize-giving.' There was a hint of reproach in the remark, but no one in the room, I'm sure, took it that way. There was cheering. Slater grabbed Adam's cup and took a long draft from it. 'To a friend and colleague, and, by the way, one of my best ever classroom teachers.' He even took a second draft from the chalice.

I've no doubt that at that moment Charlene's expression must have changed from one of jubilation to one of horror, but we were all intent on watching Slater. Then came the shrill scream. 'Jim! Don't drink from that cup!' I suppose most of the guests took Charlene's shout as no more than an admonition to her husband, a vigorous reprimand for his meddling in her ceremony. But, at that sound, I felt my blood run cold. And so apparently did Mack, closeted in the dorm with his listening device. The next sequence happened very quickly.

'Why on earth not?' exclaimed Slater. He raised the cup and swallowed once more. 'Here's hoping we can persuade Mr. Riley to come back to Hillcrest for another year, and carry on the good work.'

However, a hush had already fallen over the room, a sense that not all was right, and there was only muted applause for this new toast. Hateley, at the top end, had stood up, as if to apologise for Charlene's unscripted outburst. 'I believe Mrs. Mays is not quite herself. Please forgive us both for a moment.'

He tried to take her by the arm but she shrugged him off. 'I'm all right, Charles,' she said uncertainly, 'but take Jim and Mr. Riley to the other room.'

Dismayed silence followed this remark. Then someone said (the question exploding into the vacuum of silence), 'Why, Charlene?'

Charlene, walking down past the backs of the diners and towards Slater, said, 'I'll explain later. Get them both to the other room. Quick, or it'll be too late.' Her voice rose in a crescendo of alarm.

'Too late for what?'

And Slater, depositing the cup on the table and sitting down heavily, said, 'Uhh...what's too late, Charlene?'

Charlene turned and for a second I saw her distinctly fasten her gaze on Hateley, whether a desperate bid for help or something else I can't be certain. We were all just glued to our seats, as if paralysed.

'What's in the cup, Charlene?' It was a voice from among the guests, full of apprehension, as the onlookers became increasingly aware that the whole ceremony had jumped the rails. The question dropped like a stone into a murky pool.

'Quick!' shouted Charlene, 'get them to the other room; there may yet be time.' Strangely, no one moved.

'What's in the cup, Charlene?' A second insistent voice.

Charlene broke. Reaching her husband's side, she said, 'Jim, you're as good as dead. The chalice is poisoned.'

At that moment uproar broke out in the room, and in the pandemonium I saw Hateley steal away through the door leading to the patio and the evening sunset. Everything now, amidst the panic of the guests escaping from the room, seemed to happen at once. Mr. Slater, already distinctly pale, groaned suddenly and pushed the cup away from him, Charlene knelt down by his side, and someone (I don't know who) said, 'Quick, get them to a doctor!' and Adam too uttered a heart-wrenching groan and grasped his stomach. I was out of my chair and over to him as he slumped to the floor. I heard Charlene say, 'Jim, you fool! Why must you interfere in everything? You've got no more than an hour to live. There's no remedy for this poison.'

Slater, more from instinct than self-preservation, gasped. 'But why, Charlene, why?'

Charlene swung round in the direction of Hateley. 'It was *him*....' Her voice tailed off as she realised he was no longer there. Slater at this moment uttered a desperate groan and collapsed to the ground. There were now very few people left in the room - how many I can't say - and all shaken by the horrors they'd just witnessed, but nothing could have prepared them for what happened next. With an almost supernatural effort, Adam pushed me aside, staggered to his feet, grabbed both the chalice and the kneeling Charlene and forced the cup between her lips.

'Then poison, to thy work! Taste a cupful of your own sweet medicine at last.'

And suddenly there was Mack, bursting through the door, grabbing the chalice from Adam. Charlene uttered a blood-curdling scream, as he violently forced the remaining liquid down her throat, almost sending the cup down with it in his rage. 'Tessa, quick, go find a phone. Call an ambulance...and call the cops; it's time to call the cops.'

I left to find the nearest phone in the apartment and, by the time I returned, they'd moved Adam outside onto the terrace and laid him on cushions. He was scarcely moving and gazing out down to the prairie. I knelt down beside him, and he looked up, trying to smile. 'From where the tornadoes come,' he said softly. 'Seems like there's one coming now. It's very dark out there....Or is it the rivers? This stuff is really cold.' For a while he lapsed into silence, shifting on the cushions from time to time, as if trying to rearrange himself, get comfortable. Then he opened his eyes again, saw me there and said, smiling, 'We never did get married, Tessa. I'm sorry.' He closed his eyes and I thought he was going to pass into a coma once more, but he said, 'You know, Tessa, I once had a good friend; I never told you about him. A catholic priest I knew during my time in England. At '*Desolation Island'*.' I nodded, encouraging him, as best I could, to continue. 'He visited me, you know, when I was in Canada. My lowest moment....' Adam paused for a second and then went on, 'I once asked Father Hammond why it was they didn't allow catholic priests to marry. D'you know what he said? *'A priest can't marry a woman and God too. There's not room for both*'.' Adam attempted to take my hand. 'Perhaps it's for the best you and I didn't marry then.' I shook my head gently; I didn't understand what he meant. He beckoned for me then to come closer. 'Listen, I think I've had it...promise you'll set the record straight for me. Okay?'

Those were the last words I heard him speak. He passed into a silence from which he never emerged. I vowed I would do what he asked, but I don't know whether he heard. 'I'm bearing your child, Adam,' I whispered, unsure what else to say. He made a slight movement of his arm but said nothing. Had he heard me? I'll never know. And a few minutes later this lover of mine, my child's father, this intuitive teacher, this endlessly resourceful person, died, cradled in my arms. Was there anyone else in the world at that moment who knew what a loss was occurring here? I wanted to go with him. I could scarcely bear to be left behind. If it hadn't been for the child inside me, I would have found the goblet and drunk what was left of its lethal juice.

That's how the police, arriving in a fanfare of sirens, discovered us. Me cradling Adam's body and Mack inside the apartment, in some sort of urgent tête-à tête with my hateful brother. Were they arguing? What could the two of them otherwise possibly have to say to one another? I watched my brother, after a minute or two, move quickly across to the patio and speak briefly to the police as they approached down the walkway. I supposed they knew each other. On one occasion, my brother indicated Adam, and the chief nodded several times, and then I saw my brother hurry up the pathway towards the main school. Two of the cops sauntered over to Adam, nodded to me and cursorily checked his state, before joining their chief inside the apartment. After several moments, all of us were summoned inside; gently I propped Adam against the cushions and went in.

Everything was in disarray; cups, plates, table-cloth, strewn over the floor. Charlene was lying without moving.

'She's already dead,' announced one of the cops, feeling her pulse. Mack walked up and kicked her body hard. They cuffed him. As for Slater, he lay grotesquely, arms askew, where he'd slumped from the chair. He may not have been quite dead, but was clearly beyond where anybody could now reach him.

'Seems like he's finally run out of words,' said Mack, with all the contempt he could muster.

'Watch it, Buddy!' said one of the cops. 'You're under arrest.'

Of Williamson, or Hateley, or the rest of his thugs (Faulkner, Philips and Foreman), not a trace.

'Which one of these cups contained the poison, Miss?' The chief was already busy looking for evidence. I pointed to the goblet and he wrapped it up carefully. 'Seems like they sure had quite a little party here.'

One of his side-kicks, sensing the mood, said, 'I've often wondered what them private-school fellas get up to in their vacation time.' There was subdued laughter from the others.

'Looks like the end of one of them TV dramas,' said another, scratching his head. And involuntarily I found myself nodding.

They took Mack away in handcuffs, but he was released a few hours later when the cops were satisfied he'd had no part in the murders. The evidence on his tapes had been convincing enough for the police, and, oddly, no one who they later questioned seemed willing to recall Mack's part in poisoning Charlene. Everyone testified it had been Adam.

Later, of course, our earlier written testimony - as witness to the truth - to the newspapers became general knowledge and, in the light of that information, a guard was despatched to keep watch on the '*silent grave*' at Texoma. The ambulance men arrived a few minutes later and the chief of police, still scratching around for evidence, told them, 'These people in here sure don't have no need of medical care. Go find the undertakers and get the bodies over to the city morgue as fast as you can.' I went out again to the patio but Adam was no longer there. It seems the ambulance men had already taken him away.

And only then did I start crying.

PART III

MIRACLES

Preface

The delicate hands lingered for a moment over the motionless form below them, checked for signs of pulse, heartbeat, breathing, adjusted the valves on the intravenous apparatus, and the amber infusion began gently to flow into the inert body on the slab. The administrator remained for a while, re-checking the body and the correct functioning of his instruments, before leaving the room.

Minutes later, with a click, the flow of liquid through the tubes abruptly ceased, and save for the soft hum and the steady, feeble beep of the heart-monitor machine, everything was still.

Hours passed and the man in the white coat came back into the surgery, checked again the prone form, this time lifting each eyelid in turn and bending to look for any signs of life, or death, in the stare reflected back at him. Just the faintest smile of satisfaction registered on his face as he disconnected the needle from the victim's veins.

Hours later, dead of night, casually dressed now, the doctor returned, hauled the still-motionless body off the couch, half carried, half dragged it roughly down a flight of stairs and lifted it into the trunk of a waiting car. He drove off into the darkness.

The destination, some two hundred miles and three hours later, was a desolate lake, the night's silence punctuated by the incessant wind and lap of waves, the hypnotic croak of frogs and an occasional morning bird sensing the approach of day in the oven-hot air. No crickets were stirring yet.

The driver raised the trunk and with immense effort lifted the body out of it and dragged it towards the lakeside. But before reaching the water's edge, he'd turned left by a small rockery of shrubs and clay gnomes, hauled the body a few more heavy yards, and entered a little wooden cabin overlooking the water.

There, inside the sparsely-furnished main room, with one final giant effort he placed the inert figure on a chaise longue - a chieftain lying in state upon a funeral bier, a hero of ancient myth awaiting immolation - and, covering the shape with a blanket, departed, climbed the few steps to the car and disappeared into the on-coming dawn.

Elk Lake, October 1968

Interim

Although, in September '67, in the wake of Adam's death and burial, I moved to my parents' home in Connecticut to write up the account of those deadly events at Hillcrest, and initially sought out people who could help stave off my awful loneliness, I began, after a few months - and almost perversely it seems - to feel smothered and to crave solitude. I had already, in October of '67 - half-heartedly I have to say - started my Teachers' Certification program at the University of Bridgeport, and in May of the following year I gave birth to William, my son. Yes, William the Conqueror, a new William in the royal line, one who shortly no doubt - although not just yet - would come to inherit the sobriquet 'Bill' (another 'Bill' in the making).

Meanwhile, commiserators, well-wishers and congratulators - not to mention advice-givers within my own family - came daily in a ceaseless succession to distract me from my urgent need to write up a record of Adam's final days, and, in Adam's words, to '*tell my story*' to the world. Endlessly I feared that if I became too involved in moving forward, I would leave behind the vital details, perhaps even the main threads, of a past that needed telling, and, worse, there lay the constant fear that these gradual first shoots of a more hopeful future might just swallow up altogether my memories of Adam. I needed to keep him alive in my mind. I needed to get away.

So, in June of '68, it being vacation time at college and one year of college already completed, I left a note on the kitchen table one morning with a forwarding address, took the spare family car and moved with my baby here, to Western Canada, secluded Elk Lake on Vancouver Island. Miles from home. It may seem a drastic step, but that's what we're like in our family, given to impromptu decisions. And in truth, although I was seeking privacy and independence and time and space of my own, there was another less tangible, more indefinable reason too for coming out here: I secretly - perhaps foolishly - hoped I might just find remnants of Adam's spirit in a place where he'd spent such an important year of his life. (I suppose though that such fanciful yearnings can equally well be explained by wondering what can possibly be left, in the wake of emotional turmoil such as mine, besides a gaping void in need of filling).

I'd heard little of Mack during the ten months that had elapsed since the events at Hillcrest, following which he'd personally supervised the burial of Adam at Aubrey and been involved in the futile attempts in January of this year to bring Hateley to justice. Hateley had simply gone to ground, following his acquittal, and so too had Mack, who'd sent me just two short messages in the course of ten months, one from England, one from Mexico. He was, I supposed, searching for Hateley - Mack had never been one to leave stones unturned - but I assumed no new evidence had come to light, and I finally reluctantly realised that, without something new, Hateley would escape justice from the law. There is of course another sort of justice - one Mack wouldn't shy from - but how can one put paid to a shadow? And, besides, such a course would be fraught with danger, even for Mack. In the end, I resigned myself to the hope that either Hateley would make a mistake or that something startling would come to light. Correspondence between Mack and I had dwindled to nothing.

Then, about a fortnight after settling into my life at Elk, a letter from Mack was forwarded on to me. *Lines have gone dead...I'm at an impasse...Can I, at best, join you up there? At worst, visit? Need to get my life together again*....That was the gist of it all. It was typical Mack, abrupt, steeped in brevity and practicality. But I liked him, and my son and I would be glad of his company in this desolate and uneventful place.

He came. And he stayed throughout the summer. And I stayed too (I could take up my studies later). Summer is a beautiful time on Vancouver Island, and I could feel the spirit of Adam in these places. Along the forest paths that William and I walked, he too had walked. I knew it, felt it. Summer turned to a resplendent, golden autumn and we still deferred a decision. Perhaps we'll stay for another year.

There is nothing intimate between Mack and me, just friendship and companionship. It seems to me sometimes that Mack and I are destined to be together. William loves him, I like him, and his practical usefulness - repairing a car, putting shelves up, mending a rickety dock - I take shamelessly for granted, while the other half of me realises he's becoming indispensible. We have a small, lakeside house, a dinghy and canoe down on the dock. It's rare now the shadow of Hateley ever crosses our lives; that shadow has dwindled, and the closest we ever come to apprehension here are the night noises in the giant pine-forests that cover this rainy island. We lead a peaceful life and have free souls; I've got an assistant job at the local girls' boarding school, which will serve as part of my teaching practical, and Mack has started on a law course at the University of British Columbia in Victoria. He acts as if he plans to stay, and misses no sessions. He goes duck hunting on October mornings and from time to time joins the deer hunters up-island and is away for a night or two.

———

Elk Lake, British Columbia, November 1968

The Messenger

Things will never be the same again; the final piece in the gruesome jig-saw has now fitted into place: that murky, secretive, root-cause of those storms that blew our lives so fatally away during four dramatic years in Texas. Bill, you see, was never sick at all; he was right all along, he really *was* pursued, and had we listened, had all of us (students, Slater, some of the Board, his family even) known what we know now, things might have been very different.

One afternoon late in October I watched a tall black figure stride down the path and into the clearing beside our house. There was a certainty in his step, but, at the same time, his movements, his whole gait, betrayed a sense of deference, as though he were aware he was somehow trespassing. Strangely, even though Mack was away on one of his trips and I was alone with William, the man's whole presence left me with no sense of fear; I don't know why, because it's a lonely isolated place down here by the lake.

William was playing in the garden and I came out and met the man just as he opened the picket gate. 'Hi, you looking for Mack Neumann perhaps? Afraid he's not here right now.' I indicated with a nod the forest beyond the clearing. 'Hunting season.' I attempted a smile although I still wasn't sure whether William and I were in danger.

The black man, middle thirties perhaps, came on towards me into the garden, passing William and stopping for a second to look at him; then suddenly his whole face lit into a smile as broad as I've ever seen, the kind of smile of someone reaching at last a long-sought oasis. 'Are you Tessa maybe?' I nodded. He put his hand out. 'I'm Sam, Sam Toms.'

Again, I don't know why (must have been that smile), but I went up and hugged him, a million questions already racing through my head. Sam Toms. The little black boy in that photograph in Margaret Jackson's drawing room. The one who could complete the puzzle.

I picked William up. 'Come inside, Sam. You hungry?'

We sat inside for a while in silence, Sam looking around him, bending down occasionally and offering his finger to William, who was lying in the play-pen beside us. Finally Sam said, 'You sure gotta nice place here, Tessa. You and Mack.'

I could contain myself no longer; it was clear the man was uncomfortable and desperate to speak, to state the cause of his journey; I sensed it, but he seemed unable to find a way of starting. I blurted out, 'Sam, where have you been? Why didn't you come forward?'

He shook his head slowly, looked down at the cap on his knees, said quietly, 'I couldn't; I was too afraid. I've been afraid for years.' For a long time we sat like that, neither of us saying anything. William made a few gurgling noises from time to time, and Sam responded in some way or other, clearly relieved the baby at least had no inhibitions and could break the difficult silence. Then Sam finally murmured, 'You don't know that man.'

'Hateley?' I asked. He nodded. I said, 'I *do* know him, Sam. I know all about him. My friend Adam knew about him too. We also knew about you, the note you left Bill that day in '63, your growing up with the Jackson's. We know all that.' For a second I saw a puzzled look cross his face, but then he just nodded slowly and I went on, 'That's why we could have nailed him. We just couldn't find *you*.'

Another long, difficult silence until at last, scarcely audibly, he said, 'I'm sorry.' That's all. Having at last made the journey, this man seemed now unwilling or unable to say what he'd come to say, his relationship with Bill, what had set it all off, that secret he'd shared with Bill that afternoon so long ago The sun was starting to sink behind the pines; William was getting restless. Mack wasn't due back until late.

At last, lowering his head, as if words themselves were a burden to him, he said softly, 'You know everything, Tessa, except the worst bit, the hardest bit.'

'Then tell me it, Sam. Is that why you've come?'

He nodded and said, 'Partly.'

That seemed to release something, because the words started tumbling out, like a stream that's burst its dam. Sitting at the table, Sam told me eloquently, deliberately, graphically even, as I busied with William and his needs, how, as a child of 6, he'd been witness to the gratuitous killing of his father, crossing the dusty track one evening so many years ago in Denber.

'*Who* ran him over, Sam? (I had to keep interrupting his narrative. The questions kept exploding from me).'

'Some young rich guys out to cause trouble, down in the shanty town. They didn't stop; I guess they were mighty drunk.'

'Did you folks, you and your ma, go to the police?'

He eyed me with a gentle, unaccusing smile, as though my question was the most naïve thing anyone could possibly have uttered. And, of course, it was; I knew it, the second I'd asked it. 'You know, Tessa,' (he was shaking his head) 'complaining to the police was something we never did…not us folks beyond the tracks.'

'I guess it was stupid of me,' I said. 'Just a six-year-old boy and his mother. I'm sorry.'

Horrified, I thought for a second I'd stopped the narrative in its tracks, brought the visit to an end by my clumsiness, and I silently cursed my stupidity, vowed, if I got the chance, not to intervene again, to allow this suffering man to say what he had to say in his own way and his own time, even if it took all night. I couldn't afford to query his integrity. But would he go on?

William was quiet now after his feed; I laid him in his cot and gently tried to prompt Sam to take up the threads of his story. 'Sam, where exactly were you? Where did you witness this crime? Who else was witness?'

Luckily Sam wasn't someone to bear grudges. He smiled, nodded his head once and continued, 'My mother put me down through the hole in the floorboards, where I always went when there seemed to be danger. Pull up the floorboards and drop me into the hole, down onto the hard-baked earth under the shack where I could view to my heart's content if I wanted. Put back the floorboards….' His eyes glazed for a second, as if he were visualising the whole terrible routine, re-visiting it. Then, grinning, he said, 'Down among the scorpions and the other low-life.'

I shuddered at the thought. 'Who else witnessed it, Sam?' I repeated my question.

'My Ma. She was there. Out there on the steps….She'd gone out to see what was going on. She sometimes….'

Something at that moment jarred inside me. Instinctively, a fearful pageant was taking shape in my imagination, links between what he was telling me and what I already knew were snapping ominously into place. 'Sam, did they *see* her?' For all my good intentions, the question sprang involuntarily from my throat, prompted by what he'd just said.

He nodded. 'Yes Ma'am, they sure did. They shone the flashlight.'

I knew then what had happened. The discoveries which Adam, Mack and I had made now fitted into the puzzle, and what Sam was going to say next, I already knew. But I needed him to tell me; I needed to hear every painful detail of that awful truth. And I think Sam needed to tell it too. I could hear from the breaking tone of his voice that he was distraught and back out there under the floorboards, watching them take his mother away.

'Sam, d'you want a coffee? D'you want to take a break for a while; then perhaps tell me the rest?'

I got up and went to the cooker, but as I turned back towards the table, I saw him shake his head once and smile ruefully. 'It's been thirty years of silence. I guess that's long enough, Ma'am. I came here to tell you; that's why I came.'

But I still steered round the question he didn't want to face. 'How did you know where to come, Sam? How did you even know about us?'

He smiled, as if once more I'd asked a naïve question. 'I saw your adverts. The mention of Hateley. It wasn't difficult to find you.' He smiled again and went on, 'I've been finding people all my life. It's what I do. I contacted Margaret Jackson, my foster mother, in San Antonio. She's a good woman. She told me about you and Mack. And Adam. About your visit to her. She warmed to you.' He seemed for a second to glance round the room as if expecting to see Adam there, and I realised that maybe he didn't even know what had happened to Adam.

I said quietly, 'Adam's dead, Sam.' And as I described the events at Hillcrest that afternoon, I watched him wring his cap in his hands, as if words were no longer sufficient to lessen the pain.

Finally he murmured, 'It's tragedy in every corner and at every turn.' He lapsed into a long silence, and then I heard him say, 'A whole chapter of irremediable tragedies.'

I could contain myself no longer. 'Sam, they're not all irremediable, but why did you leave it so long?' The thought of Adam seemed to have released something in me, and my question erupted as a shout, a cry of pent-up frustration and incomprehension after all those past months, when things might have been so very different. 'Why hand an encrypted message to Bill Jackson? Why not just tell him?'

The outburst and my questions must have stung him, because, for the first time, he responded with passion and vehemence. 'I don't know what you mean by an encrypted message. I left no message. I gave him nothing which might incriminate him. I just told him, told him that all those years, when we grew up together, I'd been living a lie, that his Daddy and Hateley had murdered my Mother.' Sam gave a deep sigh. 'I even told him where my mother lay.'

'But the note, Sam? The note, with the names on?'

'I know nothing about a note, Ma'am.' He paused, and then continued, 'Anything in writing would have been too dangerous. Everything was too dangerous at that time. For him and for me.' He paused and looked hard at me across the room, as if desperate to justify his actions that day. 'Bill knew everything by the time he left me that day. I left nothing out.'

I realised in an instant that the note on which we'd based our whole search, our pursuit of Hateley, had been from Bill, not from Sam; it had been Bill who'd composed and wrapped it in code. To place us in less danger. Of course. And in that final letter, he'd pointed the way to the one person most likely to be able to crack it, Joe Verard, '*the primary Hamlet*'.

Sam was continuing urgently now, the words all spilling out in a great rush. 'It was the time of the assassination. They were all over us at that time. Hateley came looking for me that Sunday. It was the first time I'd seen him since I was with the Jackson family. I don't know how, but he'd found out where I lived. Perhaps it was all the Kennedy activity; I don't know. But I knew I had to get out, and mercifully they left me alone for one day more; that was long enough. I got out.'

I came across the room and sat down facing him at the table. There were still things I needed to know urgently, gaps in the whole sequence of events that needed filling. 'Where did you go, Sam? After Dallas in '63? I take it you left Dallas.'

'I went everywhere. I went on the run. I kind of disappeared. I was plain scared.'

'So where have you come from now?'

'I've started a law practice in California. With a change of name.'

'Sam, why hadn't Hateley come for you before '63?'

He shrugged. 'I suppose my trail had gone cold.'

'Surely Margaret would have given him your address.'

'I don't think she would have. She never liked him. Anyway, she didn't know either. I'd changed my address twice. No one knew where I lived except people I wanted to know.' He paused, and then continued, 'I'd even switched my law course. From NTSU to SMU.'

He sat now motionless except for the continual wrestling with his cap, twisting it restlessly and nervously in his hands. I could see there was still a barrier he shied away from, just couldn't cross. I said gently, 'So, Sam, tell me, what exactly did Hateley do? What is this talk of murder? What is this secret he, and all those men, are so desperate to guard?' Then I added, 'Tell me about your mother'

He didn't answer directly, took his time, as if he wasn't anxious to revisit that tale. At last he said, 'Hateley was one of those five there that night. The night they killed my Pa.'

I nodded. 'Yes, I know, Sam. The accidental killing of your father. They didn't want that coming to light.'

He responded vehemently. 'No, Ma'am, the collision with my Pa wasn't accidental. Even as a young kid, watching, I could see the vehicle veer. It was plain murder.'

We waited together for what seemed an age in that silent room, looking hard at each other, me willing him to speak, he unable to. Until at last he said, 'But there's more. Much more.'

It wasn't over. He was going to tell me. As he'd said earlier, that was why he'd come. I knew it was like a dam waiting to burst; I also knew it was no use interrupting. I'd have to let him speak. I saw his head slump, as if the weight of what he had to tell me was intolerable, and then, by a gigantic effort, he forced his head slowly up and faced me, squarely. 'They came for her the following evening. As the sun was sinking. Dark enough not to be seen; though I guess that didn't really matter to them. My Ma knew they were coming. She'd already put me back in the bolt-hole. Just as well 'cos the three of them - there were only three - entered our house, searched the place before leaving with my Ma. The truck was directly outside the shack, and I watched them pull her down the steps and tie her arms and legs in the back of the truck. They had a cloth round her mouth so she couldn't call out. And then the truck pulled away down the road, careering like a wild horse....' He stopped, eyes glazing over, re-living the moment. Then he said, 'I know, 'cos I was in it.' Amazed, I waited silently, forcing myself not to intervene. 'We came to some place; it smelled of water, musty. It was a long way from home. I remember a lot of bumping as if we'd left the track behind. I was trying to untie the ropes holding my mother, but the jolting made it difficult and my fingers were too small to move the knots. The vehicle came to a stop, and I whispered to my mother I'd wait till they were gone, and then come back and help her.' He stopped, shaking is head, as if hardly believing how little he knew. 'I thought they were going to just leave her there, dump her there, so I could untie her and then I could be with her. But no, suddenly I saw the shovel beside her and I suppose I just registered they'd come for some other reason, but I could only think of one thing, getting out of the truck, leaving Ma, coming back for her; it was my only hope. I watched from under the truck, as they dragged her to a spot by some rocks, and I had one chance then to make it to the edge of the clearing.' He paused, as if what he had to tell was impossible in words. 'They tortured her. There was a heavy shovel. They made her make little cuts in the ground, like she was preparing something at the kitchen table, but it was her own grave she was preparing; those cut marking the edges of her own grave; they'd make her go on digging until she fell in. But it didn't happen like that. One of the men - I think for sure it was Mr. Hateley - picked the shovel up from beside her, stepped back a pace and swung in an arc and struck her a blow on the right side of the head. I'm sure that's what killed her, I pray every night it killed her, and she just slumped into the little grave. '*We gotta dig a whole lot deeper,*' one of them said. '*She gotta be covered up well and good. No possum bait.*' And they busied themselves for a long time while the hole grew bigger and the light got darker, and all the while my Ma just lying over to the side, dead, and me watching it all happen from the edge of the clearing.'

Sam sighed deeply and I knew he'd relived this scene a million times already. 'What could I do, Tessa?' he asked.

'You couldn't do anything, Sam.' I sat for a second or two and then, quite involuntarily, I murmured, 'But you were there; you were a witness, Sam.'

My voice had an urgency about it, and Sam nodded. 'Yes, Ma'am, I was there.'

'Can you do something about it, Sam? Repay them for what they did to your mother?'

Another sigh. 'It's been too long now. And who'll believe me?'

'There's more evidence now, Sam. *I'll* believe you; Mack'll believe you. We found your mother's body.' For just a second I saw a glimmer of light, of understanding, flash in his eyes and then the glimmer went out. I tried desperately to distract him somehow. My questions were really irrelevant in the light of his tale, but they kept on coming. 'Sam, would you know now how to find your way back there?'

He shook his head. 'No. I never been back. I wouldn't be able to find it again, that spot. I wouldn't want to.'

'How did you get back home?'

'I walked and walked. Slept rough. Didn't dare talk to people. Some people took me in and I went on next day. And all the time my heart was heavy as a stone.'

'Sam, why did Mr. Jackson take you in? Into his family?'

'I don't know; I've often wondered, 'cos he was one of those men there that night. Maybe he just began to feel sorry for me. Or for himself. He came to our neighbour's, down in the shacks where I was living, offered her a lot of money and a lot of threats, I suppose, in order to keep them quiet. And he just took me. And they raised me. I guess the family just grew to love me, like they loved their own children.' He lapsed into silence again and his head sank, and I could tell he was rehearsing once more the dreadful, unforgettable pageant out there at the lake, no longer interested in finding ways of remedy, or of moving on. 'When they were gone, I tried to scrape away the earth, to get at my mother, uncover her, but it was growing darker and the earth just fell back from my hands into the hole as fast as I pulled it out.' He looked up at me again, seeming desperate for some sort of understanding in my eyes. 'There was just nothing I could do. Except scrape away the earth, try and expose what those men had done.'

'We *have* exposed them, Sam. We can expose them, in court.' But I knew, as I said it, that it was a lie. We just wouldn't be believed and it would raise more difficulties now than it would solve. I continued, all the same, 'Two of them are already dead, and Hateley's on the run.' I looked straight at him. 'Could you help bring Hateley to justice?'

But all he would say was, 'I don't know. Maybe.' I think Sam's will to pursue Hateley had gone altogether, if indeed it had ever existed. He'd come in order to find me, to tell someone after all these years what had happened. Now he'd achieved that, and would go back to his law firm and try to forget. As, really, we all would. The trail had gone dead. Hateley had escaped.

It was over; there was no more to tell. I said, 'Sam, I think you need to get some rest. You'll be able to see Mack tomorrow; maybe we can show you a bit of the island; it's beautiful at this time of year.' Then a thought occurred to me. 'Or stay for as long as you like. Perhaps you want to take a break from work for a bit. Would you like maybe to take a trip down to Dallas, visit with Corrie or Margaret?'

I believe it must have been my stupid mention of Dallas that sent Sam on his way; too much had happened in that city, because when I came down in the morning, there was no sign of him and a note on the kitchen table: *Tessa. I've had to go, and thank you (and Mack) for everything. If you do ever need to contact me, place a notice in the LA Times and in it mention 'grave news' and I'll know to make contact with you. I wish you and Mack peace and happiness.*

It was signed 'Sam Toms (Jackson)'. And, thus, Sam Jackson went out of my life as suddenly and unexpectedly as he'd entered it.

Elk Lake, British Columbia, Summer 1969

Rebirth

I have a silver bracelet I wear almost permanently, if not on my wrist then on my ankle (the fashion nowadays); Adam bought it for me that time in London in what must have been a rash moment of his, dropping his guard and indulging in a bit of sentimentality.

I've always loved the bracelet because of its simplicity - it suits my style - and then of course there's the emotional value attached to it, even more compelling these days for obvious reasons. There are six little trinkets on it, miniature silver creatures: a fish, a bird, a panther, a snake, a lobster, a butterfly. Originally there were seven, but the tiny dog fell off somewhere in the wilds of Texas, and I never expected to see it again, Texas being large and the trinket small. I'd pretty much forgotten the loss when, the other day, in our mail box, along with the usual few letters there lay a small padded envelope - postmark Bridgeport, date unclear - and, inside, a little gift box and inside that, sitting on cotton-wool, a miniature silver dog, a perfect replacement for the one I'd lost. The fittings, the size, were all perfect.

It wasn't my birthday; I wasn't expecting anything, and I asked Mack if he'd finally gone soft and bought me a present. He glanced at the gift, gave me one of his ambiguous looks - screwing up his eyes, play-acting the faintest of smiles - and asked me if I'd lost my senses. 'Anyway, if I'd wanted to give you a gift, I'd have given you a gift; not send it via Connecticut. What's the postmark on the inside package?'

We looked, but there wasn't one. It was just enclosed in the larger package. Mack said, 'I reckon it's from William. He likes little dogs.'

And I replied, rather hotly, 'Shut up, Mack,' and we both got on with what we were doing.

Such was our relationship; I don't think Mack had ever seen me other than as someone he could boss about, a rather insignificant assistant stage-manager at the beck and call of the cast, whether in a school play or, more recently, in a real life-or-death drama. I didn't worry; I had no stake in Mack, except as a companion.

After a while, Mack called from the other room, 'I didn't even know you had a bracelet. And why do you suppose it's not a present from one or all of your family?'

I thought for a second and said, 'I don't suppose any of them know about the bracelet either. It's not a thing I flash around. And anyway, even if they did, spontaneous giving isn't one of my family's best traits.'

'I expect then they saw your name on the initial envelope, tried to unwrap it, messed it up, put it in another one and sent it on. It's that simple.'

'Who sent it then?'

'As I said, almost certainly the baby. You love him, he loves you. He gets the privileges, you get a gift.'

Once again I said,' Shut up, Mack; it's not helping.' He was being particularly provocative, and I was genuinely puzzled, almost upset, by the arrival of that tiny silver dog. I guess Mack could have been right about my family, their sending it, but they just wouldn't have done, and, besides, did anyone know I'd lost a trinket? No, there's only one person who knew I'd lost a trinket, and precisely which one of the seven to replace....A surge of wild hope, vain and foolish, came sneaking in at the thought, but as instantly as it had come, I snuffed it out. Such senseless imaginings could prompt first distraction, second insanity.

*****

Is this little package the trigger that has prompted my sudden disturbing dreams too? I'm not prone to dreaming - I always used to leave anxious nocturnal activity to Adam, chatting as he did to ghosts in the night - but recently I've been sleeping badly too, woken up in the night by variations on one memorable tableau, a dream I can't stop from occurring. I envisage almost nightly a scene from a play rehearsal at Hillcrest, and Pete Fulton, in Act V, attempting in vain to die a believable stage death amidst our hails of laughter and derision, until Adam, eventually losing patience, throws his play-copy across the dining-hall floor, waves Pete out of the way, lies down on the concrete floor and says 'Watch'. I see it now, how realistic he makes dying seem, nothing dramatic, some noticeable difficulty drawing breath perhaps, and then, almost calmly, as if lying down to rest, he sinks back and utters a final, clearly audible gasp. It's not unlike the way he died for real that evening on Slater's patio, in my arms, and I try in my dream to close my eyes as that dreadful final sigh approaches.

But in the dining-hall that evening, we, the cast, fell silent as we watched his professional performance, and, as the seconds ticked by and the body on the concrete still didn't move, we began to applaud wildly, five seconds, twenty seconds, even a minute, until at last the applause began to die away, then ceased altogether as people started whispering, and - I remember it was Sara (always more collected than we others) - who knelt down, put her head against his chest, held it there for ages and stood up, shaking her head (nothing play-acted here) so that people began leaving the dining-hall, bewildered, because this stage death seemed to have turned into a real one. In the dream, I see Pete standing there repeating, over and over, '*My god, I think he really is dead.*' There are just a few of us remaining when at last Adam moves, sits up, gets to his feet, and laughs, as he always did when something had been well done, performed to his satisfaction.

'Mr. R,' one of us says, 'you really had us worried,' and Sara says, 'Mr. R, don't get him to do it that way; you'll have the audience walking out like we did.'

'It's only make-believe, Sara, but you need to play it as real as possible. Is Peter here by any chance…?'

…And that's it; I awake, and for one wonderful moment I really do believe he did wake up like in the dream. I'm there with them still in the dining-hall, in those carefree days; I'm swept away with a desperate hope. But life refuses to bow to mere hopes, and in my lonely bed I know Adam didn't wake up; he's gone. I saw him dead.

How long can I stand a therapy like this? I'm no longer being restored; I'm being smothered, am dying myself. Or going mad.

*****

Elk, Fall 1969

Two more months have passed, Summer has become Fall, and my dreams show no sign of fading. I'm often reminded now of that evening we spent long ago in the garden at Roanoke when the professors so light-heartedly played with the idea of identity transference, self-delusion, a spirit world beyond this one. Indeed, I came here to Elk to be near Adam's spirit, to be restored by it, but this new, capricious manifestation of him I no longer recognize. The spirit which haunts these pinewoods is melancholy, brooding, even malevolent, offering me unremitting hopes and dreams that cannot be fulfilled (how could Adam ever have endured, all alone, twelve months of this gloomy island, weighted down as he was by his own private sadness?).

I don't welcome dire spirits such as this. I've decided to leave, return to Connecticut, finish my teaching course, rejoin my family. Elk has served its purpose (if, I'm tempted to think, it ever had one).

Mack will stay on (although secretly I expect he'll be writing to join me again before long).

*****

Bridgeport, Connecticut, November 1969

I was back home here in Bridgeport by early November. I'd got my things together quickly, paid my share of the rent, leaving Mack behind, somewhat bemused but nevertheless resigned (he'd grown used by now to my hasty and arbitrary decisions). He'd shrugged as we said goodbye out there amidst the pinewoods, and said simply, 'Guess I'll see you when I see you,' and I'd replied, 'It's not you, Mack. Don't blame yourself. It's everything else.' He shot me a questioning look, and I added, 'I can't hide out here for ever; it's time to move on. I've got a child to take care of.'

I took a last, long look at the wide, silent lake, our canoes bobbing endlessly, aimlessly, by the jetty, and was sure I was making the right decision. Mack remained standing by the little house watching me go, a tall, very solitary figure, and I wondered how long it would be before he too got tired of talking to himself, living in the past and unwilling to make a leap of faith. However, it wasn't difficult to believe that somewhere, somehow, Mack would make it. His mind, like mine, was too restless, contained too much quicksilver, to remain tethered for long.

My heart was easy as I drove eastwards, the endless miles, William strapped in the back gurgling to himself. I was returning to civilization; I would throw myself into my work, complete my studies, let others take a little care of me, sleep better, exorcise redundant spirits.

But it wasn't to be; not yet at any rate. That malicious spirit of my dreams was not so easy to shuffle off.

*****

CLASSIFIED ADS STOP **CT POST** STOP **FOURTH SATURDAY IN NOVEMBER**

When I reached New England, this puzzling and challenging telegram was awaiting me, unopened. Who on earth could have written it? Knowing my address was not a particular problem; many of my distant friends knew my address; I knew my parents' address was a focal point, a clearing centre for us all. And the incident with the trinket, even though I'd put it behind me, had left me realizing that inexplicable things with completely rational explanations sometimes occur, just so long as you possess the key to unlock them. What really puzzled me about this telegram though was its peremptory tone. I just knew I'd be unable to resist its summons. That bare message understood me as well as I understood myself.

The CT Post is our local newspaper and the 'fourth Saturday in November' was the 22nd. I waited a week, bought the paper, uneasily scanned the small ads with my heart beating faster than it ought, and found at last, among the hundreds of personal ads, the unmistakable message to me: **"tertiary Hamlet on trail. Wolf spotted in 15R YP 222121010 12122211 by dulwich hamlet striker"**.

Six people only in the world knew about 'Wolf' and 'tertiary Hamlet': Mack, me, Adam, Joe, Nancy and Bill. Yes, Nancy knew, but not well enough, so rule her out. Rule *me* out; *I* didn't send this message. That leaves Bill Jackson, who wrote the original message, but who's dead, so rule *him* out. That then leaves Mack, Joe and Adam. They all knew; they all could have sent this teasing imitation of the original encoded message, so start eliminating: Mack is far too pragmatic to engage in games like this, and what could he possibly have to gain from such trivial deceit? He could have told me his intentions before I'd even left Elk. Joe Verard, it's true, had deciphered our original message, had direct access to the national grid reference system, might have fancifully re-invented the '*tertiary Hamlet*', but....

As I stood there in the 7-Eleven, a thrill of horror sliced through me, so that I had to sit down in the store, because in that instant I realized neither Mack nor Joe, supposing even their least friendly of intentions or their most fanciful inventions, could possibly have had access to the sobriquet in the telegram: *'Dulwich Hamlet striker'*. Only

Adam and I knew about that unusual nickname, and how I'd once in London, after a particularly spectacular football game, referred to him teasingly as 'the Dulwich '*Hamlet*''.

And then, I suppose, in that moment, on the stool in the shop, as I sat bewildered, almost devoid of my senses, I just knew *he* was alive, out there somewhere, impossibly, unfathomably alive, and unwilling to come forward, nervously edging out of his shell like a crustacean, and back in again, playing little jokes instead, perhaps not daring to believe, himself, that he was still in the land of the living, or understanding how.

I went hurriedly in search of the binary-coded location in the messge, working it out in my room on a scrap of paper, went up a wrong alley until I realized the code wasn't in binary at all but in base 3 (the one Bill had used in that original note), and I finally came up with 15R YP 82533 17824, a spot located somewhere in the French Quarter of New Orleans according to the national grid.

*****

I waited. I got on with my studies, tramped each day through the snow to college, leaving William in the glad hands of his grandmother, who no doubt would already be imbuing him with Shakespeare's imagery. I can't say I felt either excited or cast down by the limbo state I found myself in, merely numb; not unlike most people, I suppose, looking forward from day to day, passing their lives in a state of suspended animation, waiting expectantly for something that may or may not happen. I was however mercifully surrounded by my busy family and had little time for thinking about Adam's apparent strange survival.

The snow slowly dispersed, '69 turned into '70, the end of a decade, the start of a new one, Spring came with all its wonders. I even began to forget about that first telegram, about New Orleans, about Adam himself; it had all simply been too long, and although I knew one day he would write, send me another elusive telegram perhaps, give me an explanation (Adam was like that, methodical, predictable, delighting in tying up loose ends, but irresistibly drawn to the unpredictable too), I also instinctively began to feel in my heart we probably wouldn't meet again, that I would find him only to lose him.

Why wait for so long if he intended to come back again into my life? Deep down, however, there still resided in me a stubborn little pocket of joy at the thought that Adam was not dead and gone.

Meanwhile I told no one about his communications with me, nor about my life in Elk with Mack, and the coming of Sam. I kept it all to myself and, after all, could that really be of interest to any but the closest of friends or those tied up themselves in those events? Although I love my sisters, I can't really say I'm close to any of them - we're all too independent - and as for my brother, George, he has chosen to disinherit us from his life altogether.

And then finally came his anticipated news, first in the form of a second encoded telegram. Sent again to my parents' address. As I slit open the slim piece of paper, my younger sister gave me that look, a mixture of bewilderment and curiosity, she reserves for me and no one else,. I suppose she thinks I'm an odd-ball.

OPHELIA STOP **PICK IT UP** STOP **POSTE RESTANTE 12022210 121001212**. There it was, with that characteristic string of numerals less than 3 which I immediately recognized as the base 3 signature. As I suspected, its decoding was simple and the location very close to home: Bridgeport, Connecticut. Chrissie, my other sister, sneaked a look over my shoulder at the message and said, as I put my coat on, 'Where are you going, Tess?'

'Downtown to pick up a letter.'

'How do you know there's one waiting for you?'

'I just do.'

The letter was undated (typical Adam), but today - receipt date of the telegram - is May 7th 1970, and so I must assume the letter was written and sent sometime around this date (almost three years after his supposed death).

> …a survivor of a shipwreck, washed up on a desert island, encompassed with water. Well, not quite, but nearly….
>
> Yes, Tessa, I'm alive - which by now you've probably gathered - but how? What strange circumstances conspired to deliver me again on the

shores of life? I don't know how I came to be here, and probably never will. The actual agent of my survival will never risk declaring him- or herself. There's too much to account for, not least one empty coffin in the ground somewhere in Texas, and perhaps a gravestone with my name on it. ALAS, POOR ADAM.

In theory, I'm on the run now; I'm illegal. Occasionally I pinch myself to verify the physical side of my existence, receive positive confirmation and then journey on, a body with no identity. Perhaps I should keep it that way; it must be to my advantage that certain people think me dead.

Dearest Tessa, I woke to the sound of wind and lapping water - that sound you and I remember so well - waves against the hull of a boat. Slap… slap. I was on soft bedding, in a lake-house on the shore of Possum Kingdom Lake. I'm uncertain how long I'd lain there on that bedding - hours maybe, days even - before thoughts suddenly intruded into my inertness. 'Texoma…this must be Texoma… boats…water', and in the wake of those memories came 'Camping…Hillcrest….' Until all at once everything was flooding back, that terrible moment when I lay sinking into unconsciousness in your arms, a fierce constriction in the chest….

So I just tossed off my covering, sat up, slung my legs over the edge of the couch, kicked them to make sure I still had mastery over them, took in my surroundings, and finally stood up. A human being, upright on two legs. And then joyfully I knew I was neither dreaming, nor in some other nameless state, but somehow had survived, still had a memory intact, had been given a second chance. I crossed to the outer door, opened it, and the smell of damp clay sucked up by baking sun rushed in, the musty scent of Texas. I was still somewhere in Texas.

In fact, Possum Kingdom Lake - its watery expanses, its distant shores, its little islands, not at all dissimilar to Texoma - lies about two hundred miles west of Fort Worth, on the road to Abilene. Whoever had deposited my inert body there had perched me on a chaise longue, left me coffee, a kettle, toilet paper, basic food provisions, blankets, and 100$, to ensure presumably my temporary on-going survival.

What more is there to tell? From a newspaper shop I ascertained the date - Friday September 8th 1967. I took my hundred dollars, hired a local car and headed west, picked up, at a bank in Odessa, some money I'd had wired from England, and, because I knew eastwards would bring me back to bad memories, bad people, I kept on going, reaching the safety of California, that refuge for all strays and nameless people like myself, two days later.

Yes, Tess, I'm nameless, but you can call me Sol (for solitary) Smith. Please, for my and your security, don't show this letter to anyone, or even talk about it (I take a risk just sending it). I know I can trust you in this. There are too many people who'd be very interested to know I hadn't passed from the earth on Sunday, September 3rd, 1967. And my new identity allows me (has allowed me over the past three years) to range at liberty throughout the States, stopping here and there to check out local papers, ads in local cafes, to follow the slimmest of leads and then move on, in search of the one person on earth who would want to dispose of me. You know who I mean. I think in fact I caught a glimpse of him in New Orleans some months ago before the trail went dead.

Tessa, please forgive me if I have remained out of touch for so long. I know how hard it must have been for you, but I always knew you'd battle on and not allow the past to drag you back. You're like that; you're a winner. I hope you'll understand we cannot meet again, not now at any rate. Imagine all the questions your friends, your family would ask about me, someone appearing suddenly into your life who has a past that simply cannot be disclosed. Someday, maybe years from now, we can be together again in different, happier circumstances. I just can't be certain and can't promise anything. Besides, do you remember, one night when we were together in Gordonville, how I told you that I was like the Tin Soldier in *The Wizard of Oz*, that I had everything to give except a heart. Alas, it's still terribly true and you deserve someone with a heart. Please, don't wait for me, forget me if you can and move on yourself, have a family perhaps.

As for me, although outwardly I haven't changed - occasional shortness of breath, but nothing serious - inwardly I'm different. I feel I am reborn. I have another chance at life. Whatever spirit resides in me now is of a different sort; my Hamlet persona (or whatever it was, whatever one likes to call it) has departed, fallen off me, like a snakeskin. That obsession belonged to my old life and I am different now. I'm more at ease with myself, rid of those spirits that produce such empty fantasies and dangerous misconceptions. For now, I have to go on writing; but for *this* generation, not a new one. I believe I'm still in *my* generation; I cannot yet be shackled to another, nor to the responsibilities which come with that.

Live well, beautiful and perfect Ophelia. Please be happy.

Sol.

I stood amazed for minutes, the letter hanging from my hand. *Has he simply forgotten? Doesn't he remember? I was pregnant? Does he know he's got a son? No, he doesn't. Perhaps doesn't care. And never will. I have no address for him. He's lost.*

Thoughts and questions came flooding in, but as I put the letter down, the full realization of those stark certainties and their significance hit me and overrode any tears. And just as unexpectedly, instantaneously, I knew what I had to do: leave the United States, go back to England, forge my own life, alone.

———

August 1970, Toronto

Leaving

Are such impulses sent to guide us? As I've often re-read Adam's letter over the past few weeks, particularly lingering over the final part - his references to 'Hamlet' and obsession - I find myself wondering whether both Adam and I have not been, these past few years, so far removed from those strange, but apparent truths, which came to light that evening at Roanoke. Are we guided? Can we be inhabited by spirits?

If so, there must be now no more hesitation, no long, debilitating self-pity. Adam's right; we both have to move on. Let him then pursue his solitary, tenuous intent, the penning of dreams and the desires of others, that final abrogation of all reality. My purpose is far more rooted in the real: the care and upbringing of my son, William, whom I love fiercely.

Am I Ophelia? If so, I'll be a very different Ophelia indeed from my fictional counterpart, a stronger, freer one, a freedom bought with hard experience. I'll re-invent Ophelia.

*****

I completed my studies by the end of June, said goodbye to my family, and left for England with William. I have a cousin a few miles north of Toronto - from where I'm writing these few short notes - and in two days' time William and I will catch the liner to Southampton and our new life. I have a job and a relative in London, where I will stay until I find somewhere of my own.

Yesterday, William and I sat in the lovely sun on the grass (I spread a rug out for him) just outside the little town where my cousin lives. William crawled around a bit and then dozed off, and I lay in the lush grass, gazing at a remote farmhouse nestling in one of the small hollows of land that make up this particular part of Ontario. Not unlike England in fact, with its hills and valleys. A far cry from Texas, where I grew up. Why couldn't we have just stayed in Texas, Adam and I? We both loved the place. But for whatever reasons, it wasn't to be.

As I sat on that hillside, sucking in the afternoon heat, a small cloud passed across the sun, momentarily covering the bright fields in a cloak of solemn grey. I jumped up and anxiously spread William's comforter blanket over him. I know that up here, in October (perhaps even September), the first cold winds from the northern provinces, from the Hudson Bay, will blow across these same fields that now lie bathed in sunshine, and one morning there'll be a covering, a white pall of snow, that won't be lifted until April, even May. Could I live in a place as cold, raise a child with all the numbing hardships that go with it?

In Texas, the sun never lost its strength until well into October. Night animals still prowl down there through torrid October nights, carcasses soiling the myriad little farm-roads and tracks that crisscross each other in the heart of that wild, teeming land. Out across the entire dark stretch of it, from Houston to San Antonio, up to the Hill country of Austin, north to the three cities planted on the plain at the base of the Panhandle, west across the Brazos, lost among snaky gulches, creeks and rotting wooden bridges, and on out west into the cactus-strewn desert of Odessa, where drills dip their iron beaks relentlessly into the rich soil: across all that vast arena, creatures prey upon each other, die from passing trucks amid whirling dust, their remnants swallowed up in those seemingly endless hills and plains. And just so it is, it seems, with human life down there, an arbitrary and despotic pageant in which men too, caught up in the ebb and flow of passions, prey upon each other, man turns against man and even against himself. Such violence. How could I expose William to the possibility of violence of that kind?

I sat wrapped in memories of those days in '67 when we set out on our quest. Did they really happen? They seem now almost like a dream. Our desperate rush to Santa Fe...our uncovering of Sadie... our deciphering the code...our bold arraigning of Hateley...that final, dreadful violence in our little school on the hill. And all those deaths, the guilty and the innocent mixed up in the tragic events, the Weasel, Sadie, Sadie's husband, MacDiarmid, Slater, Charlene, Bill's father, JFK, and ultimately our young vibrant teacher and friend, Bill, his carcass too laid to rest in the Texan earth, the last vestiges of a wonderful spirit that had passed as suddenly and without warning as do the whirling tornados scouring the land each springtime and moving on....

Another cloud flitted overhead, stealing the warmth and jolting me from my thoughts. My child stirred on his blanket, probably feeling the cold. I wrapped him in the blanket and walked home, hugging him tightly.

The End

Milton Keynes UK
Ingram Content Group UK Ltd.
UKHW022328230424
441619UK00014B/683

9 798869 142658